John Healy was born in Lond
left school at fourteen. Press
military prison, he became
and lived in the world of d
confinement he became a ch
then wrote his autobiogr
received great critical acclai
Award for the Autobiography of the Year in 1988. *Streets
Above Us* is his first novel.

John Healy

STREETS ABOVE US

Paladin
An Imprint of HarperCollins*Publishers*

Paladin
An Imprint of GraftonBooks
A Division of HarperCollins*Publishers*
77–85 Fulham Palace Road,
Hammersmith, London W6 8JB

Published in Paladin Books 1991
9 8 7 6 5 4 3 2 1

First published in Great Britain by
Macmillan London Ltd 1990

ISBN 0-586-09085-1

Printed and bound by
HarperCollins Manufacturing, Glasgow

Set in Baskerville

All idealism is falsehood in the face of necessity.

Nietzsche

Buy the ticket, take the ride through tunnels of darkness. Everyone starts the journey equally safe but some will never finish it. Not bad odds when you come to think of it. Three million people use the tube every single working day.

Workers, manual and mental, Guardian Angels, Hell's Angels, nursing angels. Visitors, tourists, trippers, employed and unemployed. One great, marching, massive, frantic crush. A claustrophobic rush filters down to form at the check-out. Squeeze through just one at a time.

The crowds becoming thicker, piling up dangerously, creating a terrifying impasse around a faulty metal barrier.

A human collector, lips grimly pressed, takes over, puts out his hand without a word like Meek Pete, the silent beggar. Those that have no ticket pass coins instead. He nods, face relaxing into contented corruption.

The octopus trick won't work today. Shoot out a hand with a used ticket, left, then right, keep walking briskly through. One collector assumes the other one has grasped it. Passengers seethe, slipping and sliding, their flesh abused on those shiny plastic seats. Among all the chaos they've still got something; for the moment, anyhow, they have a seat. Others, weighted down with supermarket carrier bags, stylish high-street fads, struggle along platforms, spotted all over with grease smears like horse shit in Hyde Park. Trains . . .

What used to take five minutes can now take half an hour. Down, down, down into the semi-darkened depths. All over the capital, office staff consult their horoscopes.

Along a thousand miles of steel with a gradient of one in five, it's stuck in a tunnel by the high sign waiting for the green. Down, down, deeper, down, at last the platform's reached. Nothing in sight either way.

Wait, wait! A young woman, frustration mounting, checks the underground map.

1

Brave commuter, with a disapproving stare, suffering from vertigo. Cave memories listening for the sound that isn't there. Becalmed on the Northern Line platform in a jumpsuit, one of the worst things that can happen to a bona fide traveller. A few air ionisers wouldn't go amiss. The ground smudged by last night's revellers, varnished with vomit, leftovers from last night's picnic, the only sound the leisurely shuffle of the experienced grazer as he goes from bin to bin, content as he licks the Wimpy wrappers, stuck with sauce. Time has no real meaning here. It changes with the trains.

Pits, caves, tunnels and tubes, all uncertain labyrinths at the mercy of sewage leaks, Thames burst banks, gas-pipe explosions, power cuts, air raid, earth tremor, flood and collapse. But the show must go on. LRT has decided to give the people some sounds.

The sarge got the message from above and the buskers got it from below. One in the guts, a toe up the arse, instruments smashed. Still, the show must go on. Maestro, play the real music, please, play, play. Sounds of a summer meadow, a gushing waterfall, doves calling from a wood, skylarks twittering. Mozart's Sixth, Beethoven's Ninth or some bastard's Tenth. Nice, precise, so relaxing. The tempo's slowed to a promenade saunter. Passengers linger and loll, not in nearly so much hurry now to get out and about. The brisk natural tempo's been ruined. No one's trying very hard. Reserve melting, not a shadow of discontent, beaming with obvious enjoyment, a fast foxtrot. An old couple near the white line execute a superb little pirouette. Now the music changes, it's a rumba. The crowds shuffle gaily. A lady, closer to her bus pass than her pram, flits about, lets out a shout that might even be termed indecent. The gentle tinkle of little bells turns the tube in a mind's eye to an alpine grotto. Weary passengers shed their loads and in the space of that tender melody, become bright young things once more. Now Herr Strauss has something to say, feet press upon feet as the crowd sway, faster and faster, round and about. Watch it! Those near the edge might suddenly miss out. Slower and slower, real turns. Other sounds heard now, one tune fading into another. The vulgar waltz replaced just in time by a gentle minuet. Steps begin to lighten and they're back to walking pace, making for the exits. But now it's pop, the beat is fast.

Teenagers with well-developed thighs career down the platforms on skateboards, leap and change direction in mid air, taking the bends at furious speed. Swift swerves, that test the nerves as they spin and wheel – and slash unsuspecting travellers as they pass with with razor-toothed metal combs.

Most of the staff have been trained at 'politeness seminars' and are now more open and frank with their insults, pared and biting – got them almost to an art form. At this level anything goes and usually does.

A mixed group of men and women, of indeterminate age, depraved; skin malarial yellow, vitality sapped from years spent existing in this living tomb, let out maniacal cackles when a bevy of passengers exclaim with stifled gestures as small rodents dart between the rails.

Make shift, make do, arrows, hardboard signs, illegible scrawl chalked on a wall. Cardboard made fast with string. Passengers grind their teeth in the muted light with justifiable frustration.

In the absence of info, any noise in the lightless tunnel gives hope, however false, of approaching trains and the music goes round and round and comes out here – a speaker in a hole in the wall. The tune has a successful sound. Somebody's trying, but it's about twenty decibels above the Noise Abatement Society limit. Sets the ear drums vibrating. Passengers go north and they wanted to go south. The same tune blaring, they go up to the staff box at the end of the line. An old employee doesn't turn at their approach – one of them taps him on the shoulder. He spins round, Elvis quiff wobbling, fingers tapping the side of the box, face set in a quizzical grin, blankly staring, rheumy eyes: 'Excuse us, could you turn the music down? We can't hear the announcer speak.'

'No, sorry, it's against transport rules, to sleep here, but hold on, I'll ask old Charlie.'

3

A genuine old wino busker, one of the few left, who haven't been driven away by the trendy young professional prodigies, with broken-down shoes and frayed-edged ill-fitting clothes, was slumped over his makeshift (paper round comb) mouth organ. A young woman with tanned skin and jet-black hair stopped to give him some change, picking up, in the process, a couple of young snatchers, who got in tow following her hopefully. Buskers and charity collectors act unwitting pilot fish for the dipper sharks – a species of pickpocket, who either through injury or laziness need to have the titbit pointed out to them and lounge around buskers, apparently listening to the sound, carefully watching where those who stop to part with change keep their wallet or purse. Here they need not have bothered. Continental women have developed a way of holding their bags to prevent a quick snatch – known as the Milano Clutch, the shoulder straps secured to the forearm and gripped tightly across the chest with the fist. Perfected by the women of Italy where snatchers operate in gangs from bikes. Only way to separate an Italian girl from her bag is with a baling hook.

An old guy with a face like a crumpled newspaper, white and seamed with grime, gets a touch of the jerks, fidgeting about to ease his drooping piles – maybe a groper indulging in a little gentle molestation just to keep his hand in. Girls with sing-song voices, wind-toughened country features and masses of unruly dark hair borrow or fight over three-year-olds to use at the beg. Others, with vowels refined, get a job baby-minding. An agency sends them post-haste to Hampstead where they double up the odds when they take the kids down the tube to add credence to the bite. Kid has a great time, builds quite an appetite. Mummy's little darling's back home at four thirty, just in time for tea. Everything's getting tighter, even the soup kitchens are feeling the pinch.

Gangs of sullen jobless teenagers wander the tunnels, passageways and arcades. Black leather fingerless gloves with steel-buttoned knuckles, purely decorative. Many have served time for murder, but were released after just three years – that's cut-cost justice, guilty-plea bargaining systems. No need to beat confessions out here. Impersonal and predatory opportunists, while waiting for an opportunity, snatch off women's earrings and rip the lobes to shreds. Watch out for the untouchables – kids under ten, too young to be charged, victims of mind-wasting boredom that turns them to acts of hideous vandalism, scoop up dog shit from the pavements into plastic cartons to drop in someone's bag. Used condoms, reddish-brown-tipped Tampax, urine, dead insects, old papers, rock-hard left-overs, chewing-gum, grime, grease and dust. Awful, never clear it with the Sanitary Inspector. Plexiglass, plastic neon and chrome concrete, steel cordite, rubber and wood, harbingers of death, many have lost their lives to these in the terrible fire, others have sustained horrific injuries.

Phlegmbers – urchins that haunt the escalator areas try to outdo each other gobbing on the floor, chronic cases hold spitting contests, see how many gobs they can land on passengers' backs as they sink slowly down the moving stairs. Silence is golden – gathering and obviously hacking alerts.

The evening commuters have bottle-necked the train's door as Finn comes staggering along. He's had about six bottles too many, and plunges right in among them to fight this way on to the train. Reluctantly the crowd has parted slightly to allow a few passengers to alight. As they dribble through the small gap that has been made for them, Finn elbows forward, taking advantage of their movements to weave himself along the same path. Slots himself neatly into a small space by the door. He waits there until he gets a seat, then snatches an hour's sleep in the comparative safety of the moving train. He hadn't fancied trying to sleep on the open station where, after first being shaken roughly awake, vagrants risk being fired, head first, through the glass door by the sergeant and his apprentice. Finn often rides the Circle Line, stiff and cold, round and round, for a kip and a thaw.

The train builds up to a steady cruise but it's hot and humid and the carriage feels airless. Faces are shiny with sweat. Happily the next stop is Victoria where most of the passengers get off to connect with main line trains. Finn wakes from his nap with a start as the train stops with a jolt. Sleepily he watches the passengers flow off and on. The blacks must have got on at Stockwell. Finn can't be sure. All he knows is that he's been admiring the watch on the outstretched arm of a young woman, whose sleeveless top exposes the shaven hollow of her armpit. As she grips the strap-hanger for support, her eyes staring at the door – or maybe at nothing at all – the passengers suddenly become aware that an ugly mood has descended, and as the fierce-looking swarm of about twenty young blacks begins to stream through the train they begin to exchange uneasy expressionless glances in the darkening glass of the carriage windows.

There is something military about the way they take

7

control of each compartment, cordoning off the doors and splitting themselves up into pairs – to be able to attain the maximum results in the minimum of time. The young woman braces her legs, spreading them slightly, against the rocking motion of the train. As the black boy pulls her arm from the strap she lets out a stifled cry of shock when he wrenches the watch from her wrist. Finn, secure within the knowledge of the destitute, notices the same thing happening throughout the compartment. Wallets taken, jewellery torn off the slow-to-comply, and now and again the sound of a slap and a shout. And when it comes to their turn, those passengers who have nothing begin to fret, as if they have just been handed a telegram from the postboy announcing a loved one's death and on reading it found they haven't got enough loose change to hand him a tip.

As the track levels out the train begins to pick up speed. A young girl, hands pressed across her chest, pleads with a couple of the muggers to be allowed to keep the gold-plated good-luck charm which hangs round her neck. But the aggressor, not used to dealing with appellants for clemency, hides his embarrassment and indecision with a show of viciousness, shooting out his hand, ripping the delicate little safety symbol from her body. Her anxious boyfriend, throwing caution to the winds, makes a grab for the black, whose mate, obviously alert for such moves, lashes out catching the boy squarely on the chin with his knuckle-dustered fists. His timely aid allows his mate to sidestep as the boy falls forward, smashing his face against a notice warning those who infringe the regulations of the penalties they are liable to incur, including possible terms of imprisonment for assaults on railway staff. Passengers do not, it seems, come under its protective auspices.

With a series of sluggish thumps the train grinds to a halt. Its doors open. The horde rush off with the night's takings. Racing along the platform in one great black mass, knocking passengers this way and that in their haste to be gone.

Finn can't remember why he stood up as the train pulled

away. Perhaps it was to let the young girl's boyfriend sit down. The train tears its brakes as someone pulls the communication cord. The sudden lurch causes Finn to fall forward, missing the strap-hanger with his hand. His head catches the iron seat bar – splits open to the bone on the way to the floor. He isn't knocked out and the drink acts as a painkiller, but he feels very fuzzy and is tempted to stay where he is until the police come, hoping that he might be taken for a *bona fide* traveller and given the benefit of a hospital bed. He realises though, with sudden sickening clarity, that the law will not be too pleased about what has happened in the carriage. Urged by this thought and fighting down fatigue, he drags himself to his feet and staggers away from the train.

Carrier Bag Mary, withered, sad, and driven mad. She never meets anyone's eyes and has stopped looking at people when they start looking at her. Stoop-shouldered, head bowed, she wanders around like a crippled crab. Her eyes on the ground, mumbling aloud when she gets in a crowd. A sort of sound frequency to get them to move, keep others at bay. Her conversations start somewhere in the middle and work out towards the end, or the beginning, depending on which way her memory banks happen to be working at the particular moment, and, unless it's about money or somewhere to sleep, she doesn't seem to hear or doesn't listen to what's being said.

In the last few years the station has been her home. Before that she used to sleep in Gandhi's park in Bloomsbury. One cold November night wandering round the statue, her eyes down searching for the loose change that lovers sometimes drop as they wrestle, she caught the moon's reflection glinting from a bright shiny object. Bending to investigate she was disappointed to find it was only a Coke can ring-pull. About to straighten up she rested her hand on the base of the statue for support, getting a shock when it began to move. A closer look showed that the bottom was hollow, the back covered only by a thick piece of blockboard. The next night Mary furnished the hollow with several old coats and some sacking and she moved right in.

It's a tribute to her powers of camouflage that she managed to survive without being spotted for so long, but unfortunately her luck ran out on a night when the moon was at its brightest. A well-to-do, over-ambitious, public-minded citizen out for a walk with his over-zealous dog saw movement inside the railings of the closed park. Something was obviously amiss. Any other dog-walker might have taken no notice, let the matter drop. Unfortunately for Carrier Bag this dog-walker was Head of Psychic Studies at CELLS (Cosmic Energy Liquid Laboratory Substitutes). Even then, given his failing sight and the loss of light each time a cloud crossed the moon, he wasn't sure. But, then, not for nothing does one get to be head of CELLS. Least of all for not trusting the intuitive instincts of animals (Mary's crab-like movements having cowed the dog into a terrified bundle of whimpering fur). The man from CELLS, teeth chattering, mind a blank, sought out and beamed in to the nearest phone box. He would not have seen it either, only the dog pointed it out, straining at the leash to cock its leg in the absence of a lamp-post.

Sergeant Cuffam is not a sensitive dreamer. He's heard so many tales in his twenty-five years on the Force that the one he hears that night seems quite ordinary in comparison. Perhaps if he'd been acquainted with CELLS's latest publication and annual reports he might have shown more surprise. In the event, however, instead of scientists with laser beams, he sends two burly coppers with truncheons to sort out the park Martian.

The sergeant is merciless to sleepers. Like the end of the world, homeless dossers and winos fear his coming and tremble at his approach when he strides in among them each night to start his grim progress from the station's warmth to a cold night's penance on the streets. The only exception he makes is to Carrier Bag Mary for whom he has a soft

10

spot as his own niece is trying to become a secretary and someone has put it about that Carrier Bag once held that illustrious title. Secretaries are, according to the sergeant, a most élite group.

Nose Job, Tapper Finn, Dry Slice and Sticks Moloney sit in the station drinking a bottle. Woman glides by, a whiff of expensive perfume trailing behind.

'It ain't how you look. It's how you smell.'

Makes Nose Job lonely. 'We are trained from birth to nod, bob, duck and bow. Never touch or kiss,' he says. 'In Italy or France they embrace when they meet.'

'Women and all?' asks Finn.

'Yeah. If one girl meets ten boys she kisses them.'

'All of them?'

'Yeah. It's nothing. That's how they're brought up.'

'Sounds like a nice place if you're one of the boys.'

Over on another seat Carrier Bag Mary is talking to Italian Laura. 'You want to be careful with him,' says Mary.

'Oh, I know he's got his faults. But at least he don't piss all over my back in bed at night.'

'Well, that is pleasant,' says Mary, brightly.

A wino promised to marry Mary once and he would have kept his word only he ended up a patient on a locked ward a few weeks later.

Sticks Moloney reads aloud from a local paper. 'Says here a man bit a parrot's head off in a pub. Sod that! I couldn't do that.'

'What, not even if they was to give you a thousand pound?' asks Nose Job.

'Well, I don't know . . . I ain't got no teeth anyway.'

'You know the law's got this station bugged?'

'Fuck off. The only bugs in here are in your hair.'

They take another swig from the bottle.

'Harry's been done,' slurs Sticks Moloney.

'No.'

'Yeah. Twelve months' Pentonville. Time to catch up on his Mickey Spillanes.'

'Sod that,' replies Mary. 'Still, old Moloney's going to get money from that accident. He's only waiting for a stroke of the pen.'

'Hope he don't get a stroke of the cat instead,' says the sailor.

Fag ash and butts piled up around the No Smoking area agitate the new cleaner while the dossers won't make room for him to push his broom. He tries to listen as he sweeps, through the whirr and hum of station noise. A radio, its dial stuck between programmes. Hawk-eyed porters, hovering around to hustle tips, swoop on weary travellers.

Carrier Bag Mary, trying to tighten her string garter while rubbing herself catlike against the heating system, speaks to Eyetie Laura. The cleaner propels himself in their direction. When one sense dims, so they say, another gets stronger. Laura's shapely legs, encased in short neat skirt, knees leaning slightly to one side but otherwise directly facing him, should keep his interest while he works through his shift.

'Oh dear me, no. The last thing to do, darling, is to let a man have sex. If you can't get their money by other means I'm afraid your modelling days are numbered,' says Mary, pulling her tattered coats more firmly around her body. She is the only person who doesn't find the tube tropical.

'But I can't get through to him. He's always drunk. He doesn't seem to want to talk.' Laura had been convent educated and on leaving had known more about the next world than about this one.

A well-heeled young couple with a child walk by, bubbling with enthusiasm. They make for the seat Finn is sitting on. A disgusted look shows that he'd better disappear. They're so spick and span. He's up, off that seat and away before you can spit. Finn had been decorated for bravery during the war. Holding a position single-handed. Nose Job had had his own business. Flush Joey had done a lifer for killing a bloke. Everybody seems to have been somebody once.

Winter or summer, autumn or spring, Mo has seen them arrive in all kinds of weather. Some arm in arm, others in groups, their cultured voices carrying far on the still evening air, as, elegantly, they wend their way into the Festival Hall. Outside, the hungry homeless lie huddled in cardboard boxes, newspapers their blankets against the night's cold air, experience having taught them the futility of begging a few pence from these sensitive souls whose smiles turn quickly to grimaces of disgust at the merest glimpse of so much poverty on two legs. No nocturnes for the nocturnal. Mo turns thoughtfully – the sudden nip in the evening air brings a decision. He saunters casually after the last group of music lovers into the foyer. Looking without looking. Taking in everything, especially the coats on the coat stands. A nice blue Crombie takes his eye. He slips it off the stand, drapes it over his arm, eases over to the bar, orders a Coke, drinks it slowly, puts on the new front and leaves.

Mo's spare, almost ascetic appearance belies a turbulent history of alcoholism and prison. In the last year or so he's tried to get himself off the drink by taking up writing instead. Only then had the real problems begun. Being blackballed in the Greasy Spoon has considerably limited his choices too. Trying to avoid mixing in the field of his own addiction, keeping away from old friends – his life consists of one long avoidance.

There was the writing, of course, and he carries a notebook now instead of a bottle. His small room is littered with them – notebooks, that is. When he can't get work, which is most of the time, he steals to pay to have his stuff typed. Having lived so many years on the streets he's lonely a lot now and having a hard time getting up from that life.

Huddled in the smother he looks quite smart, heading

over to the Underground – the finest in the world, so they say. Mo wouldn't argue with that, though: it's his world, or to be more exact the place where he goes whenever he doesn't know what else to do. He never plans it that way. After all, who in their right minds would want to spend their lives down the tube? In this place you need eyes in the back of your head as well as at the front. How many blind people do you see down here? Even sightless musicians avoid it, because they've got natural instincts against dodgy areas and people, such as Rush Hour Pugh.

'Oh, just a moment, sir, there's a bit of an obstacle blocking the platform.'

'Why, thank you for your concern.'

'Yes, it's all right now, sir, this way round. That's it.' He shoves his shoulder up against the blind guy to cover his hand on the wallet. There are few blind beggars nowadays. Plenty of sighted ones, though. Mo used to do his fair share of it when he was really up against it, but his methods were crude compared with some. He'd just beam in and ask for the shekels, unlike the more sophisticated approach of confirmed devotees like Kosher Kate, who only begs young Jewish boys on the Northern Line. Nice boys. 'Have I got a daughter for you?' she purrs, immediately forging a bond of intimacy with the young male mind, only broken after she launches into her monetary needs. Not quite high finance but 10p here and fifty there. It mounts up.

Flush Joey favours a more direct approach, using a knife. Whether this is the best way or not doesn't bother Joey, he always gets money, that's why Joey is always Flush.

Old Tommy the Leaf varies the touch; not seeing himself as a beggar he helps women to carry their bags. Ask him if he ever begs them and he replies, 'I keep myself to myself.' He keeps drink to himself too. Picks up a leaf from the ground, asks a woman to give him her hand, places the leaf on it, pretends to go into a trance. Well, a minor fit. A cross between a hangover and advanced epilepsy, mumbling mysteriously, starts to give her a right load of old mumbo-jumbo. Eventually she gets too confused, after Tommy tells her she's going to fall for a tall, dark, handsome young man. Especially since she's a long-term resident in a senior citizens' home. 'I don't understand,' she murmurs timidly.

'Neither do I, but that's what the leaf says,' replies Tommy dreamily, whereupon she hands over a few bob, happy to be rid of him so easily.

The Lurcher was a good trier, always looking for a live wire. Unfortunately, a quick temper and a sharp tongue prevented him making a career of begging but he kept at it, until the time he'd had one over the eight and lurched right off platform two, down on to the rails below. He found a live wire that day, all right. Caused a few hiccups for the Transport Police.

Never, ever, beg a beggar. The poor descending on the poor. Suicide Tim standing outside the chemist administering his daily medication swallows a mouthful of bicarb from the tin he is never without. Washes it down with mouthfuls of cider until he gets the burp. 'Urrup. Farting, burping and sneezing are the nearest experiences to a sexual orgasm a dosser is ever likely to have,' he says.

Tim sticks out his tongue, asks Pugh what colour it is today. How can Pugh tell with eyes all scummed up from lack of sleep? Bloodshot, weariness and deceit.

'It's all red and pink, Tim, you're the picture of health,' says Pugh.

'Good man yourself,' replies Tim, and smiles, giving Pugh the price to go for a bottle.

'Hurry back.'

'I won't be too long gone, Timmy.' That's not his proper name, though – he's had so many cardboard identities he's forgotten who he really is.

Talking about names, Mo was riding the train the other night, swaying to and fro, loose-jointed as a puppet on the Central Line, when this smartly dressed young guy starts chatting up one of the women. The most attractive one at that. 'Would you consider me over bold', he says, 'if I were to ask you your name?'

'Sorree?' She smiles a Continental smile, so friendly it

gives a bloke confidence. Even Mo could have taken over the conversation from there.

'Oh, are you French?' replies the guy hopefully, as the train rolls along with a gentle hum. Everyone in the carriage is so unconcerned. Tired, bored even. But they are all ears. 'Yeez'. The way she says it, Mo can feel it tingling all the way along his spine.

'Which part of France do you come from?' asks the bird-puller.

'Oh, Orléans.' The word sounds like a little tune coming from her. (Mo takes another hit from the can in his pocket.) Has he been to France?

'No.' But he's thinking about going. Mo's never been either, but he's also thinking about going. He's thinking about going to Blackpool, too. It's true, every time he gets nicked he thinks about going to Blackpool.

Mo got out at Holborn. The conversation had become ordinary. The beautiful French coquette turned out to be a very young housewife, and the bird-puller a clerk in a car factory. Such observations can safely be termed by other authors as research, but for a street writer like Mo even the act of listening constitutes an occupational hazard, leaving him open to police harassment at any time.

Boring. All we want out of life is a bit of excitement. A good fuck would probably kill us all now, thinks Mo. Nourishment is the order of the day. Yet when Dry Slice Tony bought Mo a bowl of soup in the Greasy Spoon the other evening he couldn't keep it down. Spewed the lot up before reaching the door. Got them both barred. Dry Slice has not spoken to Mo since. Plenty of hostile glances. Mo daren't drop his guard in Tony's company while this lasts.

But for all his practical thoughts Mo was no more proof against sensual infatuation than the next man, the stolen coat a point in fact.

Completing his journey, Mo alights from the train. Emerging from the station he makes his way towards an elegantly laid-out square. Half-way along he stops outside a large house. Wide stone steps leading up to a fading varnished door give it a shabby grandeur. 'Selina Ashplant' says the nameplate over the eighth bell. He presses and waits. Waits for what seems an age but is in reality only seconds. Suddenly he is seized by an odd panic. 'What if she doesn't really want me to call? Perhaps she was only trying to be polite, make idle conversation. Isn't that what middle-class women do, instead of telling you straight out to fuck off?' Now he's talking to himself. Embarrassed by his anguish, about to walk away from the door, he remembers the paper in his pocket. Comforted, he reaches out once more, pressing the bell more firmly. This time he hears a step. The door flies open.

'Mo!' gushes Selina Ashplant.

He was overcome with warmth. No doubt about that greeting. Mo follows her up the stairs into a small room with a high ceiling that could have easily passed for a branch library, its four walls fitted with shelves holding hundreds of books.

'Tea or coffee?' asks Selina, in the crisp, sharp way beloved of those who make their living in the media.

'Tea, please,' says Mo, lowering himself on to the sofa as Selina disappears into the next room. As her head appears next instant through a serving hatch it was obviously the kitchen.

'Milk and sugar?' Mo wants both. As he waits for her to bring in the tea he begins checking the information he's managed to gather on the Guardian Angels for the article Selina is writing.

Selina returns with the tea, sits down and begins to indulge in gentle chit chat. For a while she is unsure of how she feels about Mo. That is, until he hands over the paper in his pocket. Suddenly becoming centred, she begins to read his notes with a concentration that excludes all else.

'Brilliant, Mo,' she cries, after she's finished reading. And she gets up quickly, making for the phone, all the time throwing back compliments at him. In spite of this, he feels anxious.

After speaking to someone at the other end of the line, Selina returns to Mo's side. 'I'm afraid I've got to go out.' He winces inwardly. Just when he's beginning to relax in her company. His look combines disappointment and surprise.

'Are you going right now?' he asks.

' 'Fraid so.' She tries hard to smile at him. 'Duty calls.'

'Oh, well. I'd better go,' says Mo, standing awkwardly. Presumably, he thinks, reporters become reporters for just that reason . . . to run out suddenly, and at the oddest moments, to look for something new to report.

'Well, I'll see you,' says Mo without emotion, having learnt to display neither fear nor happiness lest the one be prolonged, the other snatched away. He feels alone, standing in the middle of the room, but to his surprise Selina steps closer to him. So close that, tense as he was, he needs to take a step back to keep his balance or lean towards her to ease his position. But he never has to make the decision. She leans in, his breath tightens. For an instant the room disappears, he feels himself relax.

'Now I simply must rush.' Her voice breaks the spell. Mo is himself once again and within seconds is out in the street.

Down in the tube, back in his old haunts once more, idly watching the young woman walk by. The same old game except for one thing. He had held Selina Ashplant in his arms tonight and she had kissed him.

Someone is following Mo and it isn't imagination. It doesn't take extraordinary faculties of perception to realise this, because the person who is doing the tailing makes hardly any effort to conceal it. He'd noticed the man for the first time yesterday. It wasn't a vague awareness, nor a casual sighting, because the man had been walking some yards behind him, but, then, so had many other pedestrians. Those other pedestrians, however, are not behind him today. This one is. When Mo stops to look in a shop window heedlessly, the man looks into another attentively; when Mo gazes concernedly round about before crossing an empty road, the other stands casually consulting his paper. When Mo stops suddenly to ask the time, the other's shoe demands all his attention, but when he turns the corner into his own road a side glance shows that the man has continued on past.

When Mo gets to his room he peers, without disturbing the curtain, down into the road below. There is no sign of anyone. After a wash and shave he starts to write, apparently forgetting the incident – though for the next few days whenever he walks the streets he keeps looking round.

It is a small room, nothing much in it. A plastic table and chair. A bed alongside the window looks out on to the street four floors below and a small sink in the corner with a mirror above it complete the sparse furnishings. The only means of heating is supplied by two large overcoats, one of which he wears in the room when it's cold, both of which he throws over himself in bed at night.

The other rooms in the old house are much the same. All have been split down, partitioned off and reconverted to squeeze more lodgers in, most of whom are unemployed, surviving on the DHSS. The house is subject to long periods of quiet and startling mad bursts of noise. Especially during the evenings when, to relieve their boredom, most of the

19

occupants drink. When someone comes home half cut they wake the whole house, threatening to fight anyone who happens to poke their head out of a door at the disturbance. It isn't too bad if they live on the lower floors, but if they sleep in one of the upper rooms minor skirmishing threatens to break out at each landing they pass until they reach their own, which might easily take half an hour or so under the circumstances.

There are no locks on the doors. Every room has been broken into at some time or other. Now the doors are just wedged to or tied with a piece of string. Having locks would only encourage the belief that there is something to steal, tempting somebody to try. Since all that is needed is a hard push at any door, seldom does anyone bother to try.

Mo puts on his coat. He has to get out.

It's a little early for Mo to start work at the dip. Not quite rush hour so he settles down to wait. The time schedule is mucked up again, the station announcer informs all passengers, his voice dehumanised by the Tannoy as he repeats the message.

Bing, bong. 'Check front of train for destination, and if this corresponds with platform display sign . . .' Click, crackle, crunch. The Tannoy's broken down. Eyes meet only to be instantly parted, but their owners continue to observe each other indirectly.

'Best thing to do,' says Mo to an enquiring passenger, 'is toss a coin to decide your correct destination.' But the wary passenger has no intention of displaying money before the likes of Mo and walks quickly away. Mo laughs. (Have you seen the trainers they wear now? Silver strips down the sides light up neon flashes in the dark. It's a wonder they ain't got three-speed gears built in. Mind you, if they improve on them much more by next year you'll need a driving licence to own a pair.)

Mo takes another swig from the can he is never without. (As the train journeys on you may be tempted to hum. Don't. Just stare straight ahead, look neither right nor

20

left. Try not to sneeze. Avoid the temptation to fidget as this may be interpreted by your fellow passengers as some form of deviancy, occasioning glares.) He's on his own again. One minute the platform is so packed you can't even scratch, next it's deserted, desolate, a mugger's paradise. (There are many distractions, much that catches the eye, but don't be lured. Walk on, ever alert. Serene, watchful, suspicious even . . . but always keep going. Onwards, upwards and outwards. It's all been newly repaved, neat and tidy, but they can't prevent the graffiti appearing overnight. Still it's comforting to know that The Pope Smokes Dope, Fast Food Makes You Sick Quick, Lisa Benson Sucks; which football team will be victorious and which one will have to die to make them so; the most beautiful busty – and discreet – French model's phone number; which actor takes no salt; and which one takes it up the bum. Little personal details to while away the time while you wait for your connection.)

The platform starts to fill up again and the announcer has just announced that 'The train will be subject to some delay.' There's nothing more to be said, except that everything has to be said again because the sole purpose is to talk you out of blaming London Regional Transport for causing you to miss your trains, planes, appointments, dates, births, deaths and dinners. Which is bad, because the man in front of Mo has started twitching and shifting nervously at this news, and everybody, although not looking directly at him, is aware that perhaps he may be doing something obscene, unseen, at waist level or below. But it's nothing more sinister than his carrier bag rustling.

The high-pitched panting throb of the train's engines penetrates Mo's thoughts. Light flares inside the cave-like tunnel as the train emerges and rolls to a stop alongside the platform, where waiting crowds surge forward. Small semblance of politeness – even the weakest fight with all their might among a mass of writhing legs and bodies. Mo's losing ground, just managing to avoid being trampled underfoot, bumped hard again, but with his face stuck in someone's armpit, knee wedged up against another's groin,

21

he claws his way back to find himself wedged between two businessmen. Quick halves of bitter still linger on their breath. Unyielding briefcases knock threateningly like predatory animals against Mo's legs. The tallest starts speaking, his moustache bobbing up and down.

'Central Finance have done a nasty, slapped a D Notice on us.'

'Good heavens, never,' replies his shorter, tubbier, companion.

''Fraid so, old man.'

'When?'

'Yesterday. Tomlinson was three sheets to the wind when Finestart Consolidated phoned to ask Records whether they should sell fast or slow. Old Tom told them to go fuck themselves, and hung up.'

'Good Lord, whatever's going to happen next?'

'Well, in my humble opinion,' says the moustache, 'and of course I'm willing to listen if I'm wrong, Myers, Sidwell will try to get together as soon as poss to form a merger, before Central can do likewise and float all the other major companies.'

'My God. Myers, Sidwell is part of my consortium. Where does that leave me?'

'Well, yes, exactly, one can't help wondering. Hope I'm not being over dramatic, old boy . . . But . . .' He tenses as someone wrenches open the window. The air pours into the carriage. It is reviving and cool.

With soothing murmurs the train slides to a halt at Bank. Mo alights and makes for the Northern Line. Gliding along to get the feel of the crowd. In that ebb and flow he touches without touching and rubs without rubbing against tender female flesh, until male and female become one great human mass. Fused together by their hectic, hell-bent, one-way, lemming march-or-die movement.

Mo boards the Edgware branch. He knows every twist and turn in this tunnel through the earth. And when the tube, in taking a curve, gives a sudden violent lurch, he's ready, his nimble hands quickly inside the unbalanced passenger's pocket, purse or case. He steps off at the next stop, tosses the empty wallet in the bin as he pockets the crisp notes and heads for the exit escalator.

He emerges from the tube into the lovely warmth of a summer's evening. He strolls along, every so often stopping to gaze into an antique-shop window. You'd never see Mo doing this a few years back. Stop in any posh area for more than a minute and the police would have pulled him in so fast on sus his feet wouldn't touch. They'd still be doing it too if the middle class hadn't pushed the poor out of the thrift shops by abandoning their sharp expensive clobber for more neutral jumble gear. What a turn up for the book it used to be before the Old Bill got used to the sudden fashion change, having just fitted up some spotty adolescent who turns out in court to be Lord So-and-So's nephew, or Lady Skitherington-Blythe-Bluntington's son.

Selina Ashplant is not surprised at Mo's voice when she answers the phone. (Like most people from small middle-class families she prides herself on her egalitarianism.) Certainly a good writer. But he was so . . . so . . . socially clumsy. She doesn't want to appear shallow but there will always be the class thing between them. His failure to grasp this is clear in his voice.

'Have you got a suit?' she enquires.

'I'll get one. I can get one easy.'

Selina smiles to herself. His eagerness is fetching. Amused and confident, she teases, 'Have you ever had a suit?'

'Not really,' says Mo slowly. 'They're too cold.'

'Cold?' She laughs, sharp and taunting. 'But what do you wear when you go the theatre or to a restaurant?'

Mo is flustered. 'I don't go there a lot,' he mumbles. 'I go other places.'

'Really?' she queries. 'Where do you prefer to go?'

Desperately seeking something with which to impress her, Mo blurts out, 'To hear classical music. The Festival Hall. Them kind of places.'

Mo does not seek to become bourgeois but a bright mind and a good brain cannot alone elevate one from the lower depths. An ill-equipped gladiator in a highly professional arena, he needs some security in his life. Less desperation, a bit of affection.

'Would you,' he asks quietly, 'care to go with me one night?'

'Well, I would like to be able to say yes. But I don't know . . .' She hesitates, searching carefully for words. 'Oh, it's not just the suit. There's all sorts of other things—'

Mo blunders on. 'I could get some tickets—'

'There's your missing teeth.' She cuts across him sharply.

25

'Have you ever considered doing anything about them?' Her voice fades.

'Rome wasn't built in a day!' says Mo. 'And they'll hardly trouble anyone because I know when to keep my mouth shut.'

Suddenly she drops all her teasing composure. She does not know what more to say and is glad he cannot see her face . . .

Mo wakes late, springing from his bed to wash and dress. He leaves the house quickly in a mad rush. He is hoping to reach the offices of the Department of Social Security before they become too crowded.

In the heavy air that smells of poverty, of mental and physical illness, Mo waits, hoping to sort out where his Giro is. Like dozens of others, trying for the rent not a visit from the man. Every so often the voice on the Tannoy calls someone to their doom. (Here, the Tannoy never breaks down.) Babies screaming, children playing subdued games around adults with subdued faces – faces lined with a thousand disappointments, borne up only by the weekly Giro.

Mo joins a queue of people on the right-hand side of the room. Those already interviewed sit to the left, visibly more relaxed, their poverty already proven, impatient to be gone. At last Mo's name is called. He goes to Cubicle B. The interviewer is a big young guy, with glasses, wearing a sloppy pullover and jeans. Looks like a dosser. Speaks like a politician. Gives Mo the old 'we-know-all-about-you' penetrating stare before opening up his folder.

'Terence Morgan? Age thirty-eight? Address 402 Bishop Tutu Street, formerly Queen Victoria Place? Now what, you may ask,' he says, 'is the significance of these red stars which are embossed on each page of your file, Mr Morgan?'

Before Mo has a chance to reply, he goes on. 'It's this. These red stars tell us at a glance that we are dealing with a problem file.' Then taking a pipe from his pocket the clerk lights up before continuing. 'Yes, yours has become somewhat suspect.'

'What do you mean?' asks Mo.

The clerk stares at Mo coldly. Then, in a more formal tone replies, 'Mr Morgan, please try to refrain from interrupting

27

while I am in the process of explaining your position to you.'

'Yes, but I don't get what you mean. I've been waiting two days for my Giro,' says Mo, as a dense cloud of pipe smoke nearly suffocates him.

The clerk banks up his pipe before replying studiedly, 'Sadly, the clerks here often behave badly. Much of the time they can be offended by the slightest irregularity. Unfortunately your irregularity could not be classed as slight. This is the reason for the delay.'

'What do you mean?' asks Mo, in a voice charged with emotion.

Without giving Mo a glance the clerk proceeds as if there has been no interruption at all.

'It's a frame of mind, of course, that the unemployed psyche themselves into before making claims, and the more outlandish, false and naïve the claims, the more positive and determined their frame of mind.' He puffs at the pipe and another cloud of dense smoke seems as if it might seriously damage Mo's health.

Mo's worried. The man in the next cubicle is just finishing his interview, or that's how it sounds, as his voice comes through the partition. Then, the noise of a chair scraping as he stands up. Mo turns slightly to watch as the man walks over to the exit, his shoulders bent like someone who has just spoilt their last chance.

The clerk leans over towards Mo conspiratorially. 'Ah, but that is not the case with your claim, Mr Morgan.' His voice seems to have a reassuring note, as though whatever Mo has done will, eventually, be overlooked.

Relief starts to show on Mo's face as the clerk continues, 'There are hundreds upon hundreds of claims to be considered here today, one or two of them straightforward, a few of them honest even, yet there will inevitably be many thousands of them false, with the result that the clerks are forced to consider all claims as potentially dishonest.'

'So what's that got to do with me?' shouts Mo, more in fear than in anger, 'Where's my Giro got to? That's all I came in here to find out.'

'All in good time, Mr Morgan. All in good time. You see, we have received information that you are working. And furthermore—'

'I'm not working,' roars Mo. 'Where did you hear that?'

The clerk continues, unperturbed by this outburst. 'We have received information that you leave your house every morning from Monday to Friday to catch the tube, and at 7 p.m. you alight from the tube to walk along Ramsden Street to your home.'

Mo is flustered; he suddenly remembers the man in the street. Of course he is not working in the usual sense, and needs to avoid any connection with the tube and prove his poverty, he starts to deny all that the clerk has said.

This had led to a very violent shouting match, with Mo having to leave sharply, just before the police arrived. Well, that was yesterday, and yesterday's gone, mused Mo, now safely ensconced in the caff, having a meal and a cup of tea. And until he can satisfy the DHSS that he is not working, he is going to have to work even harder down the tube. Not that the tube is some kind of cesspool, which has sucked a load of social inadequates down into it spawning some kind of low- life subculture; there's nothing sinister about it really, it's just a natural state of affairs – much like the government's plan to retain rogues among their élite in nuclear shelters when the bomb drops. And after the bomb? They'll all emerge children of the ghetto.

Nose Job Kelly's reading an American book. *Successful Business Techniques*. Found it in the litter bin. Sticks Moloney's spoken to him twice but got no reply: he's testing out 'The Delayed Response Method', which as any city gent knows is the art of not getting lured into anything. Sad – because Moloney's walked off with the drink since he got no reply. Pity Nose Job hasn't reached page two, which is 'The Art of Spontaneous Response to Stimuli and Sound of Every Kind'. Verbal. Non-verbal. Signals. Hand and foot. Traffic signals. Body signals.

Old alcoholic sailor rolls by, listing to port.

'What's his body saying?'

'Nothing, just too much weight in the right-hand pocket of his overcoat.'

'Even out the weight, Jack, 'fore you get a tug.' (Tug is slang for pull, like in arrest, by over-zealous Transport Police.)

He tries to get rid of the overcoat because it makes him look too sussy. And he's liable to get a tug. Sell it for the price of a drink. Some mug will get a bargain and be able to brag about wearing the real thing.

Paul, the educated drop-out, gives Sailor the price of a bottle for that coat. Then, draped in the coat, gets a tug from two bobbies. Fairest in the world – who quake when they hear the languid cadence of expensively educated designer dosser speech.

'Sorry, sir, just routine. We thought you were a working lad.' They genuflect themselves out of sight.

'Just two very bad tailors, can't even pick an easy fit-up lately,' thought the sergeant wearily as they continued on patrol. Catching Nose Job with the book.

'It's only a book about business methods, sarge. Found it in the bin outside.'

The sergeant doesn't care what it's about. He doesn't want winos reading on his station. 'Possession is nine-tenths of the law. And you've just proved your case. Let's go.'

So there they sit, all bunched up together on the station's benches. Shoulder to shoulder like the mutant survivors of a nuclear war. Missing eyes. Missing teeth. Missing limbs. Flush Joey. Old Tommy the Leaf. Sticks Moloney. Suicide Tim. Scotch Jimmie. Edinburgh Ann. Sexy Sonia. Italian Laura. Shakespeare. Tin Legs. Jacko. The Gadgee and Teasy Jeannie.

Piercing smell of urine. Thoughts on cheap wine. A young woman walks by. Never look at anyone or they'll look right back.

'Have you got a light, please, love?'

'Sorry. I don't smoke.'

'Don't put yourself under the spotlight, Sticks.'

'She's got a nice posh accent, though.'

'So what. You don't think with your voice.'

Shuffling Eric wanders by. Face smashed up and a damaged eye. Been helping police with their enquiries again.

You can say where you're going, but not where you've been. Flies circle the open wounds on their heads. In the morning there is only sickness.

Carrier Bag Mary shuffles by. They call out to her. No reply. Anastasia's become anti-social trying to trace her antecedents. A chorus of racking coughs fills the air. Some winos take half an hour to clear their throats of solid wastings. Wet clothes. Wet shoes. Wet brains. In the absence of brain cells winos are guided by alcoholic instincts. Moloney begs a guy for a smoke. Guy gets nervous, runs away. There's a fine line between begging and demanding with menace.

Italian Laura is a relatively new face in Hell. At twenty-one a bit of a beauty. 'Charges ten quid a go,' says Tapper Finn. 'So you can tell Laura you love her, but you can't fuck her for economic reasons.' He starts laughing. It turns into a coughing jag and from that to a minor fit. One more little drink. Tomorrow they'll give it all up.

But Hell is selective. Its denizens are beginning to snub Mo more and more, something he had of late tried to ignore, hiding his warmth behind an aggressive manner to push their hostility aside. Spies, traitors and defectors would be familiar with that feeling. It is as if he'd committed high treason, giving up drink. Stories are being bandied around of how he's holding out; becoming too up-market, mixing with another crowd.

Contrary to popular belief, a policeman does not have to have an enquiring mind, he needs a *creative* mind. In the absence of suspects, guilty parties, facts and figures, someone has to invent them. Justice must be seen to be done. Live bodies found, produced, confessions extracted, trial dates set and met. Any body, pulled at random off any street, fits the facts of any crime perfectly. And therein lies the art, thinks the sergeant. *Real* art. Not the poncy stuff that writers, painters and playwrights pass off as art – come the revolution, he'd have *them* all inside.

'OK,' says the sergeant to the assembled coppers in the Briefing Room. 'This is important stuff so leave the teas alone and try to get your heads round it. This is straight from the Assistant Chief Constable's mouth, B Division – I'm going to bring you right up to date. It's that time of year again,' he says, starting to read from the document in his hand. 'Foreign gangs of pickpockets are expected to arrive in London this week to prey on tourists. Interpol has indicated that the numbers are likely to increase this year. This is because of a blitz on crime in the New York subways and the Paris Métro. Some of the gang members are from Latin America and are identifiable by scars on their hands, sustained during the most severe form of pickpocket training on clothing which has had razor blades sewn into the pockets.' This is received with low appreciative whistles.

The sergeant continues without comment. 'As in American football, gang tactics are fearsome and carried out with cool precision. They utilise numerous set moves. Using the guard's button on the outside of the train a member of the team prematurely closes the carriage doors. One set of doors is then held open by an accomplice, causing the passengers to squeeze through into the compartment. As they do so, wallets, purses and valuables are lifted. Sometimes on the escalators a team member presses the emergency stop button, whereupon an accomplice will work his way through the built-up crowd below.'

One of the young constables is rash enough to interrupt with a question. The sergeant impatiently waves him into silence. 'The number of offences on the Underground has soared from 999 last year to 19,999 this year. And that's only the ones that get reported. Since February this year there have been more than 1598 cases of pickpocketing. 349 robberies – sixty-six at knifepoint resulting in eight killings, and half a dozen hand-gun incidents. Muggings are the fastest growing crime, requiring the least skill. And as we all know, muggers are generally failed pickpockets. However, mugging gangs have developed styles all their own. They include "crowding" – a passenger in a nearly empty compartment will be surrounded by six or seven gang members. They will engage in pleasant conversation before making it absolutely clear that passengers have no choice but to cough up their cash and jewellery. Then there is "taxing". This consists of a gang working their way through a carriage taking valuables from each passenger. "Steaming", the notorious strategy of mass invasion of a group of travellers by a gang that indiscriminately robs anybody in their way.'

A keen-eyed young constable trying to be an old soldier pipes up, 'Yes. Nearly all of them carry knives now. The most common is the—'

'You want to come out here and tell us all about it?' says the sergeant caustically. 'As Constable 281B has so aptly reminded us, most of them do indeed carry knives, the most common being the Barracuda knife, a serrated implement with a seven-inch blade. They've also started to use whistling codes to send messages through the tunnels, warning each other of approaching officers or likely victims.'

In an excess of diplomacy, perhaps not wishing to spoil his men's confidence, the sergeant omits to tell them that the clear-up rate for crime on the Underground is around 19 per cent. The most recent success was the arrest and ultimate conviction of a couple of litter louts, eighty-five fare dodgers, and a gang of drunks, one of whom had been urinating on the emergency stairs, and two who had been spitting.

'OK,' says the sergeant casting his eyes around the room. 'Got all that?' Heads nod as they begin pushing back their chairs. 'Hold it,' he says, suddenly shaking his head, 'Just one more item. I nearly forgot.'

A loud 'Aaah' goes up in the room.

'OK, OK. Settle down. A report has just come through from divisional HQ that while travelling during the rush hour several young women have reported to railway staff that chunks of their hair were found to be missing on arrival at their destinations – presumably removed en route.'

This news is greeted by the coppers with loud laughs and whistles. 'I know, I know,' says the sergeant. 'You don't miss a slice off a cut loaf. But keep an eye out all the same.' The Underground's like that, thinks the sergeant as the room begins to empty. In any other place there would be some reasonable explanation for the mysterious phenomenon that keeps cropping up. But not down the tube . . . Oh no.

The cold bites deepest just before dawn. Finn awakes from his drunken slumber, curled up like a dog in a shop doorway. His head throbs as he makes his way towards the tube for a warm-up and the chance to thaw his stiffened limbs. Rain has begun to splash from a grey sky. The day is already turning out to be dreary and cold as he pushes open the glass-fronted station door. A blast of hot air wafts over him. He flops on to the nearest seat. Most of the seats are occupied at this time of the morning by the homeless, who, slumped wearily around, lips blue, faces white with fatigue after a night on the streets, are trying to suck some energy and life back into their frozen bones. Of course they know this cosy state of affairs cannot continue for long. The police, generally the last to arrive if you need them and the first to appear if you don't, will soon be along in the form of the sergeant and Co. Still, is happiness not happiness because it only lasts so long? Finn looks round for his mates – the Old Firm. There they sit, all bunched up together on the station floor, backs against the wall, shoulder to shoulder, genuine survival experts. At this time of day they don't look too formidable.

The station is starting to get busy. The white letters begin to appear like giant domino dots on the face of the massive black indicator boards, falling into place with loud slapping sounds. As Finn gets up to go over to the lads, Tommy the Leaf goes by, assisting an elderly woman with her luggage. Struggling with her case and his hang-over, thinks Finn, as he listens to the woman harping on at Tommy, with withering precision, her fears of missing trains and excess baggage. As Finn joined the lads, Sticks is begging passing passengers, using ploy number one, the standard approach of the beggar's itinerary. 'Have you got a light, please, guv?'

It's a waste of time asking for a light. Better to beg straight out for money, thinks Finn irritably, faced now with the prospect of standing for hours watching people go by in the heat or wandering the streets alone in the cold.

By 10 a.m. the sergeant has not appeared to chase anyone away, or to arrest those out on leg bails – committal warrants by their name. Everything seems to be turning out well until Dry Slice Tony, who'd disappeared earlier on, reappears as if by magic, right in the middle of the highly gleaming station's central concourse floor where it's a crime for a dosser to be seen, never mind tread. Passengers begin to slow down, others stop altogether, as they become aware of his antics, scudding drunkenly about in the middle of the tiles, like some demented ice skater. All this unaccustomed limelight must have gone to his head (or more correctly his stomach) and without a thought for the toil and care of frequent polishings, he spews his guts all over it. Finn turns away in disgust, mumbling to himself, 'I can't stand prima donnas.'

Uppermost in Finn's mind, as he heads down the escalator to the platform, is his need for an undisturbed sleep. And to this end he needs to beg. The long straight platform is empty and silent except for a couple of big well-fed businessmen who keep pacing back and forth – sentries, with furled umbrellas shoulder high. Finn finds a quiet spot between two platforms to relieve his bladder. In the absence of toilets down below, some people are forced to create those puddles of bright watery reflectors seen from time to time in alcoves and apexes.

His face is grey with tiredness, his cheeks seamed with strain. Shreds of pink puckered flesh, surrounded by hair, peep out from the labial gash on the side of his head. His latest wound throbs mercilessly from the loud screeching of train brakes each time one pulls to a stop. As he finishes his pee and moves away, someone gives a violent sneeze. Finn jumps, swearing in embarrassment at the state of his nerves. Like so many others who live on the streets he never seems to catch a cold. But, then, colds and flu are luxuries that only those with warm rooms can afford. He staggers a little as he makes his way along the platform to the seat. He's not had any proper sleep for about a week, since being thrown out of the hostel.

He'd paid the mandatory week's money in advance and was particularly bitter at not being given a refund, having damped the mattress on the first night. He puts his hand to the cut on his head which is becoming very itchy and sore, stifling the urge to scratch, consoling himself that these symptoms are the first signs of healing. He remembers suddenly that he'd been sitting on this same seat yesterday. He remembers the posters too, urging him to take his holidays in the Mediterranean, put his savings in the Woolwich, and that the only obstacle to his girlfriend having a Big Experience of Bliss was a little bottle of perfume.

Finn begins panhandling passively at first, the prompt extension of his hand without a word, but the first person he approaches brushes roughly past him. Still, the best thing to do when refused is to steam right into the next person you meet, before your nerve has a chance to go. His next victim is a businessman, complete with brolly and bowler. May be ex-officer, Brigade of Guards, thinks Finn, trying the man with an ex-private, ex-infantry yarn, to which the man's reply is a series of nods. But as his expression does not change throughout, Finn cannot be sure whether he's been listening or not. He would have started all over again if the arrival of a train – which he is not really sorry to see as its departure will leave fresh begs – had not forced him to end it. He is just about to walk away when the man suddenly thrusts his left hand into his jacket pocket, and brings out a couple of coins, drops them as if they are tainted into Finn's quickly outstretched hand and, without a word, moves swiftly forward, boarding the train just as the doors begin to close.

Finn is confused by the sudden glut of possible begs as the train draws away, being left with only the slowest straggler of the group. He moves in. Tireder than he thought, Finn's tone soon begins to indicate that he is very weary. Letting his story drift, giving too many useless and irrelevant details, until the passenger, becoming tired, moves off without a word. He couldn't have messed it up more if he'd tried. He sinks on to a seat. Even beggars need a little rest sometimes. After a short spell he resumes his work. As soon as he sees a face that looks sympathetic, cheerful, happy or kind, he beams in. But along with bad weather, late trains, broken-down escalators, increasing fares, strikes and industrial action, he's viewed as just another hazard. With practice, after the first few words, it's possible to tell the ones that'll never give anything. But his experience is shot to pieces from fatigue. The next few passengers fob him off quickly. He begins telling longer, and what he hopes are sadder-sounding tales. Even when they show no inclination of putting their hands in their pockets he keeps talking, thinking that they might eventually relent and all his previous efforts would not have been in vain. He stops trying to judge people's charitability by their faces. Letting chance take a hand instead, he approaches them at random, but his luck is no better with this system either.

The platform becomes stifling. He begins to sweat. A picture paints a thousand words. Finn decides to come in from the front, face on, directly, hoping this will allow them to adjust to his plight on sight. After a few tries, although he has no better luck financially, he feels he's receiving a much better response. His new manoeuvre consists of walking casually in front of a passenger and, as if by chance, turning his head slowly to meet their eyes, unguarded at that precise second. This enables him, he contents himself with the thought, to form a clearer judgement of his chances before moving in. Every now and then he affects a little stutter, hoping to stoke up at least a spark of sympathy. However, he soon begins to realise the flaws in this system, swiftly abandoning it when the passengers' trains begin to arrive before he's got half-way through a sentence. Every artist needs some form of recognition; most produce their best work with encouragement. Beggars are no exception, their need being more immediate, though. Finn sits down on the platform seat. He checks his earnings. Twenty pence so far. As he returns this untaxable income to his pocket he notices Mo coming along, stopping every now and then to exchange verbals with some of his old platform pals, to whom arrivals and departures have long since lost all meaning. Moving between two worlds now, Mo soon reverts to the actions and banter of the streets.

There's an announcement over the loudspeaker. 'We are sorry to inform passengers that owing to flooding all trains will be delayed temporarily. Normal services will be resumed as soon as possible.'

Dotted all along the platform's whitewashed edge, tired and edgy commuters stand clasping their briefcases and bags, newspapers and mags. In downcast and unstirring little groups they listen attentively as the announcer repeats the message.

Mo weaves his way up to where Finn sits.

'Flooding? We ain't even had a shower for over a month. What they on about?' he says by way of greeting, and frowning thoughtfully he sits down. Playing at being a concerned citizen.

Finn's thoughts seem much simpler. He spits on to the rails and searches his pockets for a match. 'When the train's late, what they going to say? Sorry we regret that passengers may experience some delay this evening because the police have just pushed some poor drunk under it,' he replies tartly.

'Leave it out. It's only the tube,' says Mo, his eyes squinting more from the need to urinate than from any mental puzzlement.

'Yeah, but whose tube is it, eh? Don't ever let the law know you're down here looking for live wires, or they might introduce you to one.' Finn lets out a cackle that passes for a laugh. Finally a train pulls into the platform with a cold blast of air. Some passengers, among them a large black man in long flowing robes, alight, winding their way through an immobile maze of others bunched round the train doors.

'Excuse us, chief,' calls out Finn as the black man is about to pass them.

'Yes?' The man stops. He has a friendly manner.

'Could you give us a light?' gestures Finn, a cigarette butt to his mouth.

'Oh no. Sorry. I do not smoke.'

'OK, thanks all the same, chief,' croaks Finn glumly.

The man looks pensively at them, taking in their scruffy, destitute appearance. 'Would you be offended if I offered you some money?' he asks kindly.

They brighten instantly. Finn is dumbfounded by this unsolicited gift. Mo starts laughing.

'Offended? Oh, that's a good one, chief, you couldn't offend him if you hit him with a fourteen-pound club hammer,' smirks Mo.

Finn laughingly takes the money from the man's out-stretched hand. 'I could lose my bus pass over something like this. Get thrown off the social,' he scolds, shaking his head in mock concern.

'If you had one . . .' chides Mo.

The man looks puzzled. 'What is this "social"?'

'It's our benefits, chief,' says Finn, at the same time nudging Mo in the ribs conspiratorially.

'Benefit? What is the benefit?' queries the man, looking pointedly at the two of them.

'Well . . . they're sort of everything you need to get through life in this country,' answers Finn, with a sigh at having to give the man such a condensed breakdown of the social services.

The man looks up at the indicator board. Slowly, under-standing seems to dawn on his face. He beams. 'Oh, benefits is like God? Yes?'

'Something like that, chief,' say the lads giving him a crooked smile.

'Do you make sacrifices to god of benefits?' asks the man, beginning to fall in with the humour of the street.

'Oh yeah,' says Mo, laughing. 'We sacrifice our whole life to them.'

'But how is this possible?' The man winks. 'You are still alive. When our forefathers made sacrifice young virgin was killed.'

'Well, I suppose being on the social's killed one or two.

But they're not too keen on virgins, chief. They'd rather give to couples,' says Finn.

'With many papooses,' adds Mo, laughing.

They all laugh, each aware of the futility of it all.

'But benefits in the end is good. Give you everything and take nothing.' The man is trying to keep the humorous momentum running.

'Oh, it doesn't exactly take nothing. There are other ways of being dead, chief. Like losing your working independence, freedom of movement, what way you are allowed to spend your day or night.'

They all appear subdued by this.

'Well, I must be going home. Look after yourselves,' says the man, shaking his head. 'Benefits.' He looks round, puzzled. 'Who knows what powerful forces are at work down here?'

Finn's head jerks up at this. 'The only powerful forces at work round here, chief, are the police,' he says darkly.

Mo laughs. But the man is unsure now. The mention of the police seems to have had a sobering effect on him and he waves them goodbye.

'There's some very nice people about,' says Mo, watching the man's back as it disappears down the platform.

'Yeah. They're so nice, I don't know what they're doing down here,' replies Finn, rubbing at the stubble on his face.

'Yeah,' he continues. 'It's nice to be nice. But not too fucking nice.'

Mo shrugs.

A train mourns in the tunnel, shattering the silence a moment later as it bursts into the station. Not many people get off, but there's quite a crowd trying to get on. The queer thing is how they all persist in boarding the train through the same door, while a couple of yards away another door is clear. In twos and threes the passengers begin to dribble past. One, a young woman, is carrying a wooden carving in her hand. It arouses Finn's interest.

'That's a nice bit of sculpture you've got there, love,' he

calls out. She looks at him with an offended expression. Obviously a tourist who's misunderstood. Finn's peeved. 'When I was in North Africa,' he continues, 'I looked in a doorway and seen this girl making something better than that. She had to concentrate really hard on what she was doing too.'

'What was she making?' asks Mo, continuing to watch the woman's curvaceous body disappear down the platform, fascinated by the tightness of her dress and wondering what she wore underneath.

'I don't know,' says Finn, without turning his head. 'But when she had it finished it was gorgeous'.

'Marvellous what they can do nowadays,' replies Mo. Looking round at Finn heedlessly he goes on, 'I think I'll go up the Helping Hand. Try and get a cup of tea off them.' He makes as if to rise.

'I was up there Tuesday when they gave out the soup. Vile it was. Tasted like rubber,' says Finn, screwing his face at the thought. 'Oliver Twist wouldn't have wanted seconds. Once they used to give out soup with lumps of meat and red and green things bobbing about in it.'

'Sounds nutritious,' replies Mo, absent-mindedly eyeing the newly swept platform. They stand out against the cleanliness of the place, tending to blend more naturally with litter-bins, toilet washrooms and refuse tips.

'I don't know about that,' grumbles Finn irritably, 'but after you'd drunk it you could feel it slurping around inside, doing your guts good.'

'Healthy stuff,' chirps Mo cheerily, sitting back on the seat.

'Yeah. You knew you'd got something down you after it.' It's hard to tell by his tone whether Finn is happy or saddened at the memory.

'No need for an overcoat, eh?' harks back Mo, baiting Finn cheekily.

'Yeah. Kept the heat in all right. I used to be as strong as a bull after it.'

'Go on,' says Mo sarcastically.

Finn gives him an old-fashioned look. 'Yeah, so strong I could snap a twelve-stone bloke's neck like a twig,' he says, making a screwing movement with his hands to emphasise the point. Finn is flash, in a harmless sort of way. A leftover from his years in the ring.

Mo laughs. 'Well, fucking good job I'm only ten and a half.'

Finn is a little taken aback by this. 'Yeah. Well, you're out of the danger zone,' he says as a train bursts out of the tunnel, slithering to a stop.

They watch the passengers jostling each other in their haste to get on and off. Some well-dressed passengers go by, talking to each other in shrill accents.

Mo spits. 'Funny, ain't it?' he shouts, to be heard above the noise.

'What?'

'This mob down here. All lah-di-lah, posh voices.'

'Yeah. And them posh voices always seem to be in charge of them without posh voices. Like nick governors,' laughs Finn.

Not only nick governors, thinks Mo as he continues to watch the struggling commuters. 'You know they never used to travel further than the length of their own village in Saxon times,' he says.

Finn tilts his head thoughtfully at this before replying, 'Well, they never had free bus passes them days, did they?'

Mo grins. 'Well, I'd better get moving,' he says, again rising to leave.

'What sort of stuff do you go in for nowadays, then?' asks Finn.

The question makes Mo sit down again slowly. 'Oh a bit of this, a bit of that. You know. If anything's on offer I'll have it,' he replies, settling himself comfortably up against the tiled wall.

'I've been weighing something up down here,' says Finn, lowering his voice. 'Might be a right little earner.' He looks around cautiously to see how Mo is taking this. 'Course I got to plan it all out yet.'

43

'An earner, eh? Down here? You got something on then?' asks Mo, pretending interest for the sake of talking but, more importantly, to avoid any later criticism from his peer group.

'Maybe. Maybe not,' says Finn with considered vagueness.

'I thought you said you knew an earner,' replies Mo, trying to pin Finn down like a frustrated butterfly collector.

'I said it might be,' corrects Finn.

'Aah!' is all Mo can come up with.

'You, ah . . . fancy doing it, then?'

'Doing what? When? And where?'

'Oh, something. Within the next week or so.'

'I'm not sure. Got a lot of stuff on myself at the moment.' Mo will never be shot for over-eagerness.

'Like what?'

'Oh, you know. This and that.'

'Very tight schedule, eh?'

'Sort of. Got a lot of appointments coming up,' says Mo grandly.

'Important, are they?'

'You might say that.'

'Mornings or afternoons?' Finn asks quickly.

'What?'

'Your appointments.'

'Oh. Ah . . . neither,' replies Mo, flustered now by Finn's probing. 'Phone calls. Timing. Being around. That sort of thing,' he adds, nimbly recovering his ground.

'Sounds like you've got a lot of time to pass in between,' says Finn, sarcastically.

The constable and sergeant appear at the other end of the platform. They saunter slowly in the direction of the two lads, who pretend not to notice their approach, feigning normal conversation in spite of the considerable effort it cost.

'What are you two waiting for?' asks the voice of the sergeant, doing away with any pretence.

'A train,' replies Finn innocently, but with gleeful relish.

The sergeant, taken unaware by such an obvious answer

to his leading question, takes a good half-minute to recover before continuing more deliberately. 'Someone robbed the chocolate machine last night. I'm looking for a name.' He waits expectantly. 'Well?' His voice demands more than enquires.

'How about Mickey Mouse?' barks Finn, with the casual bluntness of the streets.

'You trying to be funny, you fucking paraffin lamp?' snarls the sergeant, his hands bunching into fists.

'No, guv,' says Finn, tactfully in a low voice, immediately regretting his former insolence.

'You'd better not be,' says the sergeant quietly. He doesn't appear angry or menacing — but he isn't falling about laughing either.

'See that you catch that train. We don't want to find you two here when we come back.'

As they walk off the constable remarks to the sergeant, 'They seem to like being lippy.'

'Yeah,' says the sergeant. 'They seem to like it so much that sometimes we have to call the ambulance for them.'

Mo's surprised at Finn's unguarded outburst, and says so. 'No good trying to give them smart answers when you're down on your luck, and you ain't had no proper kip. Better to act stupid. That's your best chance to avoid a good kicking. Course you may still get a good kicking but at least you'll have the satisfaction of knowing that you never provoked it. And you can put it all down to bad luck.' He finishes, looking pointedly at Finn, wondering whether he's trying for a free bed the hard way and not wanting to get roped in himself.

'Yeah. There's a lot of that floating about down here lately,' says Finn. He pauses to watch the antics of a young child scolding her mother for not buying her something from the machine.

'It's getting harder to find a quiet spot to kip in since Suicide Tim and all them other panhandlers started jumping about.' He shakes his head wearily. 'Half the nut-house seems to be down here now ever since that new Mental Health Act deal.'

'Suicide Tim? He's clean off his head. What happened to him, I wonder?' muses Mo thoughtfully.

'What difference it make? Everybody's mad to some degree. Only thing is some got their shit under control more than others.'

Mo feels rebuked by this somehow. 'What's he do now?' he asks, doggedly.

'Same as before, trots round rummaging in dustbins,' says Finn, fumbling in his pocket for a butt.

'Not much future in that,' nods Mo dejectedly.

Finn shrugs, 'Not much future in anything. Anybody wants to see the future, all they got to do is look in the graveyard.' He laughs hollowly.

'That's true. We're all born, and we all die. It's the bit in between most of us have the trouble with,' says Mo, screwing his face and mouth into a grimace.

'Yeah. The bit in between opening and closing time,' laughs Finn, eyeing the new cleaner sweeping the platform nearby.

Mo is impelled to laugh too. 'What's that earner you got on, then?' he asks noncommittally.

Finn, still watching the cleaner, replies, 'Yeah, I suppose I could use you on it. You've got a quick smile and you don't let your face stay all twisted. Straight people like that. They don't feel uncomfortable around a bloke like that. Then they're not on their guard.' He pauses for a moment. 'And that's everything when you're working with nothing.'

'In other words, I look sincere.'

'You could win prizes for it,' gestures Finn openly, with honest, upturned palms.

'What's the score then?' asks Mo as a train pulls in with a loud choked roar.

Finn keeps quiet until it's possible to make himself heard without shouting. Then replies smugly, 'I'm going to stall the lift at Hampstead tube station.'

'You what?' exclaims Mo.

'Course, I'll have to fix the electrics first,' he continues importantly.

'You couldn't fix a battery in a pocket torch,' replies Mo disgustedly.

'Cobblers . . . When I was in Burma with the SAS—'

'Don't you mean when you was in Brighton on the DHSS?'

At this they go for each other, sparring around. Then get frightened. ''Ere. We'd better pack it up in case the Old Bill come back,' says Mo, struggling to keep his nerve in the face of Finn's sudden tigerish stance. Finn agrees. They sit down again, getting back to the conversation from which they had strayed.

'What do you mean?' asks Mo, pretending to breathe evenly as if the sparring had cost little effort. 'Stall the lift? Where's the earner in that?'

'In the goodwill,' says Finn, breathlessly.

Mo gives him a look of bewilderment before replying, 'In the goodwill? Whose goodwill? The fucking law when they catch us poncing about with railway property?'

'Naw. The passengers, when we happen to be the first on the scene to open the doors and let them out.'

Mo thinks for a while about this before replying. 'Yeah,' he says reluctantly. 'Maybe. At least they couldn't refuse us if we begged them for a few bob after that.' He pauses as another thought occurs to him. 'How we going to stall the lift in the first place, though?'

At this a smug expression crosses Finn's face. 'A little pebble in between the runners of the door should do it nicely.'

Mo's head jerks round like a puppet's. 'Naw. You're joking. Big piece of technology like that. No way.'

'Funny, though, how a little bit of nature can sometimes fuck up a big bit of technology.'

'I don't know . . . a pebble . . .'

'Ever had one in your shoe?' asks Finn shaking his head, as though that decides the argument.

Mo looks thoughtful, nearly convinced that Finn's plan is workable, if only in theory. Suddenly his face takes on a sly look. 'What about the alarm?' he says, happy with his cleverness at spotting the possible flaw.

Finn's jaw tightens. He pretends to pick something up off the floor. Mo watches him steadily, saying nothing. Finn, puzzled, tries not to look at him. Mo starts to rise. At that, Finn speaks. 'A bit of chewing gum stuck in between the hammer and the bell would take care of that,' he says, continuing in a matter-of-fact voice. 'So, we'll do it between five and six one evening.'

'Here, that's rush hour,' hisses Mo.

'Yeah. Handbag and wallet time!'

'Fuck that. Them crowds take up all the oxygen. Stacks of negative vibes. I won't be able to breathe.'

'Don't worry me. I can make one unit of air last five minutes. Seven if I'm really on form,' says Finn, giving Mo a suitably mysterious look.

Mo is flabbergasted. 'Here, you sure it's only lack of sleep you're suffering from?'

'Yeah. I don't deny it. I could really do with a kip. But then again, what I'm on about is even beyond that if you're really practised up proper, like.'

'What is?' asks Mo, more than a little surprised at Finn's little esoteric detour.

Finn cocks his head sideways, listening to the station's familiar purr.

'Yoga.'

'You what?' asks Mo, neither surprised nor puzzled by this, thinking he's heard the word wrong.

'Yeah. Read all about it in the library last winter, after Rush Hour Pugh let me in on the secret. And I'll tell it to you, if you like.'

'What secret?'

'Yoga,' says Finn, glancing at his feet. The tiles round the seats are worn slightly more than those on the rest of the platform.

'Yeah, but what is it?'

'Nothing. What is is. And what ain't ain't.'

'That it?'

'Yeah. That it!'

Mo's quite baffled by this.

'Yeah, I know how you feel. Took me several months to

get over the shock when I first became enlightened,' adds Finn flippantly, without batting an eyelid.

'Yes. Anyone can see you're out of place down here,' says Mo, staring sideways at Finn's haggard face. He looks at the passing passengers, the coats of the newly arriving ones showing signs of dampness. Raining outside, he thinks. The hair of those standing directly under the artificial light is moist and shiny. It reminds him of cold winds, wet pavements. He's glad to be underground.

A woman ambles along the platform stopping in front of them. They watch her with interest. She's young and pretty in a flouncing mini dress, irresponsibly and haphazardly showing all her charms. Catching the intended and the unintended in its swirling arc. She turns away, annoyed, suddenly aware of their awakened lust, and moves closer to another passenger whose extraordinary height and somewhat friendly little half-smile more than reassures her. (The Snipper is very pleased to find some minutes later as he follows her on to the train – long hair bouncing – that it is very crowded.)

Finn yawns. 'I wish there was somewhere I could kip.' He stretches, tired and jaded.

'Yeah. You're knackered at this game without sleep,' Mo sympathises. 'I'm OK myself in my place but there's not enough room to sneak anyone else in . . .' His voice trails off.

'It's OK,' says Finn. 'No good being together when one's on and one's off the drink. Still, if I get hold of a few more bob I'll book in somewhere myself. Anyway, now I'm going to try and have a kip in the pisshole.' He turns, eyeing the cleaner standing in front of them, holding a plastic bag with his left hand while filling it with rubbish from the shovel in his right. Shrivelled apple cores, brittle orange peels, Coke cans, sweet and chocolate wrappings, newspapers, dust, dirt, fluff and grime. Finn wonders if the cleaner ever finds any money.

Mo interrupts Finn's mental inventory. 'Right, be lucky,' he says, rising to his feet, and moving off slowly in a pair of brogues which do not seem to be his own.

Finn, left alone, goes through an unmarked door into the staff toilet. Later, when the cleaner comes in to check the cubicles, the locked door, together with muffled snores, gives Finn away.

'Come on. Out of there, before I call the police,' thunders the cleaner, banging loudly on the door.

After some indistinguishable sounds, the chain's clear flush is heard and Finn comes out, bleary-eyed. The cleaner, broom in hand, watches Finn disdainfully as he staggers by.

The sound of a departing train's engines echoes back mournfully as Finn emerges on to the platform once more. He stretches his tired bones before defiantly lying down on the platform seat. Gradually, fatigue overwhelms him and, oblivious to commuters' stares, he gives in once more to sleep.

'Oi! Wake up!' The voice jolts Finn. 'You know you can't sleep there,' shouts the cleaner.

Finn stares, stuck between sleeping and waking.

'Come on! I've already told you.'

Finn rises stiffly, mumbling. He staggers away along the sparsely occupied platform as the voice on the Tannoy informs of yet another delay.

Finn forces himself alert. Looking for a face. The platform is not too crowded. The few people that are on it look very anxious. Not a smile to be seen on any face. The result of the previous announcement, thinks Finn. It's going to be difficult to find a good beg among them. He notices that his hand is shaking. He feels embarrassed, baulking each time he attempts to approach someone. It isn't a question of swallowing his pride. One discards pride when the situation in life makes it useless. He's simply too ill and too tired for begging today. Still, when you're desperate for a drink or the price of a kip, shakes or not, you have to get on with it.

A well-dressed woman, looking rather less bitter than the

others standing about, encourages Finn to move in. She has one of those faces you think you've seen somewhere before. It takes every bit of strength he's got to make him go up to her. She looks at him, taking in his ragged appearance with about as much joy as a drill sergeant in a military prison.

'Excuse me, lady.' She is slightly surprised that he means her. 'I'm not trying to chat you up or anything like that,' he adds.

'Really,' she says, eyes hovering between amusement and curiosity, as if she might know quite a lot about men chatting women up but not so much about those who didn't.

Finn is flustered. 'No, I'm a seaman, you see,' he says, in a tone implying that seamen are above everything and anything unconnected with the sea.

'Sounds like you've got quite an exciting occupation,' she replies. One worker to another, like.

'Ah, yes. Trouble is though I've lost me money and all me documents.' When the woman makes no reply, he goes on. 'But if I could get to Tilbury I could get a ship,' and with a pretence of honesty he clumsily turns the pockets of his jacket inside out.

'Well, I don't think this is the most direct route for Tilbury,' she tells him, helpfully.

'I know. I wonder if you could help us, lady . . .' he stammers.

She stiffens, visibly, the suddenness rather than the vagueness of the request making her immediately alert.

'In what way?' she asks cautiously.

He pauses, but her homely face inspires confidence and he continues, '. . . with the fare,' he says, matter-of-factly.

She looks suspiciously at him. The station has started to fill up again with new batches of released office workers. Finn is growing uneasy. 'I'm sure I'd get a ship if I could get there,' he suddenly blurts out, jolting his head as a nearby passenger shakes out his paper with a rustle. It's easy to see his nerves are on edge.

The woman starts searching her bag as she speaks. 'You're obviously in a bad spot. I'm going to trust you not to spend this money on drink,' she says, giving him a piercing look as she hands him a five-pound note.

Finn can hardly contain his delight. 'God bless you, lady. I won't buy drink. I don't drink much anyway. I'll get a bed straight away with it.' She looks sharply at him. Realising his mistake he adds, 'I mean a berth.'

She smiles with affectionate encouragement. 'Well, goodbye. I hope everything works out OK for you.' A train rumbles to a halt with a long, loud, labouring hiss of tired brakes.

'Thank you very much, lady,' he calls back, loping off towards the exit escalator. With the vitality that only money can bring, he wonders what the smart young man-about-town in the advert does with his old suits when he's finished with them.

At the local hostel, in a queue of dejected, scruffily dressed men, Finn is second at the booking-in window. A big, rough, bouncer-cum-attendant-cum-bed-checker looks on threateningly. The receptionist, a similar type, is about to book in a gaunt, decrepit, old man without looking up from his desk.

'Next!' he roars.

'Two nights, please, sir,' says the old man, humbly proffering his money.

Suddenly the bouncer lets out a violent roar. 'Here, here! What's all this? What's all this?' The old man begins cowering with fear. 'He's not coming in here, Mr Burgess. Oh, no, he's a damper,' says the bouncer, laying emphasis on the last word.

Everyone seems shocked by the word.

'What? You despicable wretch,' says the receptionist in mock disgust. 'A damper? In this hostel?'

At this, the bouncer grabs the old man by his coat collar, making more fuss than necessary. 'Come on you, out of it,' he puffs, hustling the old boy out of the door. Turning round he dusts off his hands. 'I never did, in all my life,' he says, glaring threateningly. 'I can sense 'em.'

The receptionist, very impressed by his colleague's ability to spot undesirables, is not slow in complimenting him either. 'So sensitive. You're gifted, Mr Scott. Like a diviner.'

'Yes, Mr Burgess, and I don't even need a rod . . . Two kinds I can spot right away. Dampers and stroke-pullers.'

'Like that scoundrel last night.'

'Yes. I knew he was going to go for that other slice.'

'You moved fast there, Mr Scott. Oh, yes . . .'

'You've got to be alert. Keep your wits about you for stroke-pullers. Spoil it for everyone they do,' replies the bouncer self-importantly.

'Yes, I'm afraid you're so right, Mr Scott.' He looks at the ragged queue with a show of weariness.

'We try our best . . . But how are we ever going to sort them all out?'

Mr Scott does not wait to find out.

'We do indeed, Mr Burgess,' he growls, running his eyes over the men threateningly. 'But when everything else fails, I find that a good kick in the crutch will often do the trick.'

Mr Burgess does not appear surprised at this somewhat unorthodox method of tuition.

'I suppose you're right, Mr Scott,' he says, thoughtfully. 'With a little less mollycoddling and a bit more discipline, who knows what might be achieved? Instead we subsidise their addictions. Handing them this, giving them that. Allowing them such high-class accommodation at such low prices.' The thought of it all seems to be too much for him and he shouts out angrily, 'Right. Come on you lot. Next!'

Finn hands him the five-pound note. 'One night, guv'nor,' he says, dropping against the window with fatigue.

The receptionist looks at Finn for a second, as though he might reject him. Then pushes a ticket at him, with his £3 change. Finn pockets the coins quickly and starts to walk off.

'Oi! You!' the bouncer roars, stopping Finn in his tracks as he is about to walk away, pointing at the counter where Finn's bed ticket still lies. 'Ticket!' he says, glancing at the receptionist with a show of exasperation, as if he pities Finn's forgetfulness, yet at the same time feels nothing but contempt for it.

Finn, too tired to care, picks up his ticket without a word and makes his way towards the stairs which lead to the beds. He climbs four flights to the top of the hostel, enters a dimly lit room with seven beds in it, five of them occupied by fitfully sleeping men. Finn grunts wearily, takes off his overcoat, and places the contents of his pockets under the pillow. After this necessary precaution he climbs under the blanket.

He lies awake for a while, hardly conscious of the coughs and groans, belches and moans of his companions, as he relishes the security and anticipates the luxury of a whole night's undisturbed sleep. But relishing or anticipating is not doing. So, suiting action to thought, he turns over contentedly and peacefully he dozes off.

Finn wakes sluggishly the next morning. Pushing himself up slowly on one elbow he peers around at the empty beds whose occupants have already long since risen and left. He slides his hand under the blankets, a disturbed expression coming to his face and looks quickly at the bed nearest him. It has not been slept in. Struggling out of his own bed he slips smartly into the one beside him just as the loud chimes of the hostel bell ring out for breakfast. As his head hits the pillow the raucous voice of the bouncer is to be heard. Without breaking the momentum of his stride he enters the room.

'Come on, you lot. Out of them pits!' he roars, even though it's obvious Finn's the only one in the room. Finn begins to go through the motions of rising as the bouncer moves swiftly from bed to bed, deftly ripping the blankets back.

The bouncer's mood seems more cheerful than that of the previous night. The catchy tune he whistles seems to bear this out. It isn't a rondo, nor a minuet. Neither is it a waltz. Perhaps it's a little sea shanty that makes him happy as he works. Yes, the anchors and mermaids tattooed on his big, hairy arms, along with a full rigged ship on his bare chest, seem to bear this out. It's quite a pretty tune, deceivingly dainty in comparison the bouncer's vulgar looks. And in other circumstances, perhaps, Finn might have started tapping his foot. But at that particular moment, Finn, his back to the bouncer, is tying his shoelaces. Suddenly the tune comes to an abrupt stop, to be replaced by a very unmelodious shout.

'Who slept in this one last night?'

Finn turns his head slowly to look at the bouncer, whose face has now become twisted with fury.

'I don't know, guv. I was asleep when they all got up.'

The bouncer looks fixedly at him as he volunteers this neutral piece of information. And without withdrawing his menacing eyes replies, 'Bloody damper!'

Finn is too cunning to fall for this cheap dosshouse worker's trap, returning instead to the tying of his shoes in preparation for the day's wanderings.

He mumbles, 'Yeah, they're dodgy all right, guv. Spoil it for everyone they do.'

Still fuming, the bouncer picks up the pillow from Finn's old bed. Stopping suddenly in mid curse he asks, 'You sure you don't know who slept in this one, then?'

Finn stands up, longing to go, and yet he lingers. 'No, guv. As I said, I was asleep when they all left.' The bouncer's eyes light up at this.

'Well, he was a gentleman, whoever it was. He's left a tip for the dormitory manager.' And picking up the three pound coins he drops them into his pocket.

Finn's face freezes in shock.

A poorly dressed youngish man, with a dragging limp, winds his way in among the rush-hour crowd. A checked peaked cap pulled far down over his forehead partly conceals his damaged eye. Supporting himself with a stick he slowly edges his way in among a bunch of businessmen, just as the train screeches to a halt. Everyone bundles forward, blocking the passenger getting off in their efforts to get on. One person out of step snarls the whole lot up. The doors close. The train pulls away. The passengers settle down. The limping man slides his hand tentatively inside the nearest businessman's coat. Feeling for the wallet. Suddenly the train lurches the wrong way. The Limp withdraws his empty hand. The businessman looks suspiciously at him, taking in the other's badly scarred face and eye. The Limp stares straight ahead, feigning innocence. The train stops. Some passengers alight, but a more considerable crowd get on. Limp's hand accidentally brushes against a young woman's bag. He can hardly believe his luck. Gently he opens the bag, takes out the purse. But this has caused his hand to become wedged against the woman's leg. It's an intimate position. He does not dare – nor care – to move. Besides, movement would only spoil the moment. It ends anyway as the train suddenly enters the station. She squirms and draws away, deftly sidestepping around him to get out. Before he was injured in the Falklands War, the Limp had been in bomb disposal and after his discharge had seen no reason why he should not continue to earn his living with the delicate touch.

Next night on the Central Line everyone struggles and bustles with bags and baggage to board the 4.55. It's all so difficult and Limp is part of that difficulty. Among that teeming, humid mass he spots her in a dress that clings, provocative and planned, showing breasts and bottom not to be touched by office boys or lower ranks, her bearing seems to say. Limp gets in behind her. She has the most beautiful face. Where else but down the tube would Limp ever get so close to such a gorgeous creature? Pushing, pulling, tugging, gouging, the workers force their way on board. Breathing in each other's breath. The dense oppressive heat brings out stale whiffs of odour, cloyed sweet with perfumes from bodies forced together by that crazy, swaying rhythm of the rush-hour waltz. Caressing her softly – such thighs, such hips. She seems not to notice as Limp's hand explores the contours of her perfect shape. Now she's begun to fidget, but the moving hand slides on. Boldly over a firm thigh, guided by the panty-line. Coming to rest gently – accidentally, even – up against the pubic mound. There is no sound, no struggle. They have reached a silent truce. Limp holds the position until he feels her bag pushing slowly against his hand. Trying to pry it loose from her plump sex. Lurching, swaying, he jockeys for position until he feels her fat purse below.

The lights dim, then flicker up, as the tube grinds to a halt between stations, its engines idling, drawing big asthmatic breaths. Each minute seems an hour. The passengers start to fidget, shifting their weight from foot to foot, trying for a more comfortable pose. The air becomes stale, hot, as they shift more vexedly about. Everyone unyielding, no one's giving ground. The pretty gazelle finds she is trapped and cannot move. The train starts up with a shudder of annoyance. She gets restless, fidgets about, struggles harder, shifts her body, but Limp's hand stays gently wedged between the unbelievable warmth of her firm thighs. The train rattles on. Finally she stops struggling and looks at the Limp. She looks him right in the eye. He looks right back. Brazenly holding her angry gaze. It's a battle of wills. If he takes his hand away now, he can never put it back. She is growing uneasy, finally looking away, trying to seem unconcerned as if everything is normal and nothing has happened.

But something is happening. She is sliding her bag against Limp's hand again, trying to pry it loose, but this time he doesn't touch the bag or go for its contents. It's her warm, soft, female bulge he is after now, with no thought of money in his head. Leaning in a little to offset the motion of the train he turns sideways on and rubs his hand over her firm mound. She remains seemingly unconcerned. Docile even. He has won the battle of wills. Until the steel cage reaches a stop her secret place is his.

'So the Snipper's a fetishist, then?' says the constable to the sergeant as they go about their rounds.

'No. That's where you're wrong, constable,' replies the sergeant. 'You see, technically he's a thief.'

'A thief?' replies the constable, wrinkling his brow.

'Yep. That's what it's still classed as on the statutes. Theft.'

'But, surely,' says the constable, turning to look at the sergeant steadily and evenly, 'there's quite a considerable dividing line between a thief and—' He got no further.

With a look that does not invite further interruption the sergeant snarls, 'I don't care who's doing what to whom. One of the victims was some upper-class guy's daughter. Now we need a body to take a plea. Or we're going to get it ourselves . . . in the neck,' he snaps, irritated by his bold underling's persistence. They have nearly completed their rounds in silence when suddenly the sergeant brightens.

'Now. He looks like a wrong 'un,' the sergeant indicates, pointing at a small bald-headed man, standing near the gents. The man gives a worried frown as the two upholders of the law approach him. 'You waiting for something?' asks the sergeant casually.

'Yes. Yes. I am actually. I'm waiting for a friend. We're going on to Camden Town.' The truth is more embarrassing. Hanging about in toilets to avoid the cold while waiting for the midnight soup run.

'Not tonight, old son. You're coming with us.'

'What for?'

'Loitering outside a toilet with . . . ah . . . obvious intent,' shrugs the sergeant, as though that answers everything. His delicacy is touching.

'Intent of what?' asks the man flustered.

'To procure a minor, or minors, for sex. Let's go.'

And they do. Up to the first floor where the constable had thought he'd seen it all but under the sergeant's auspices is yet to see more.

'Start getting soft with them and you can kiss law and order goodbye,' mumbles the sergeant as he steers his prisoner up the stairs, through the police station door and on into the interrogation room. He waves his hand at a chair indicating to his prisoner to sit down.

When the constable (who'd left them on the landing to fetch charge sheets and statement forms) comes into the room, locking the door behind him, the sergeant relaxes. 'Do you know what a nonce is?' asks the sarge, leaning over the prisoner's shoulder from where he's placed himself behind the chair.

'I've not heard the term,' says the prisoner in a voice drained of emotion.

The sergeant looks at the constable. 'He's not heard the term,' he mimics. 'Well, no matter. You'll become most familiar with it by the time you've finished your own term.'

'But I haven't done anything,' says the prisoner, squirming to look round at the sergeant.

The sergeant makes no reply, allowing the prisoner to build his own intimidation out of the silence. 'Yes. It's a dodgy old charge that,' he says, after what he considers adequate fear-building time has elapsed. 'Yes, real dodgy, trying to procure minors for sex, with or without verbal or physical approach.'

'But I haven't done anything,' pleads the prisoner, throwing his arms in the air with frustration and making as if to rise.

'Sit down,' roars the sergeant, pushing the man back into the chair, at the same time leaning further over to stare into his face.

Repelled by the coldness of the sergeant's eyes, all the fight seems to flow out of the prisoner and he flops down heavily, head bent. The sergeant, looking at the prisoner's bald head, shining in the glare of the 250-watt light, clears his throat noisily. 'OK, constable,' he begins. 'Let's have some action or we'll be here all night.'

'Right, sarge,' replies the constable dutifully, without really knowing exactly what line of action the sergeant has in mind.

'Particulars, constable. Let's get some down. Otherwise we might be accused by the Board of Penal Reform for holding suspects without due consideration of the first name niceties advocated by some probationary officers as judicial etiquette, necessary to enhance police cultural reform. Don't want cells full of nameless ones. Although we've got plenty of homeless ones.'

After completing and confirming the prisoner's social status and particulars the constable moves on to more personal details. Description of clothing, looks, build, height, weight, scars.

'Sorry?' says the weary prisoner, failing to hear.

'Distinguishing marks,' interrupts the sergeant.

'Oh, yes. I have.'

'Well,' prompts the constable, 'what are they?'

'Freckles,' beams the prisoner, striving to please.

A sudden violent blow on the back of the neck causes him to flop forward head first, hitting the floor.

'One of your dizzy spells?' says the sergeant, grasping the prisoner by the shoulders and hoisting him back vigorously on to the chair.

'What happened?' asks the prisoner, groggy with shock, eyes wandering from the sergeant to the constable.

'There's no time to go into details,' quips the sergeant.

The prisoner shakes his head as if to beat his memory away from the whole affair.

'OK,' says the sergeant, inhaling deeply as if sucking up the last ounce of patience he's got left. 'Charge him.'

Although the man hadn't actually been doing anything wrong at the time, he isn't naïve enough to believe that he won't be in serious trouble if the sergeant goes ahead with his intention of fitting him up on a sex charge and, flustered by fear, begins wildly protesting his innocence once more.

There was never any doubt in the sergeant's mind about his next move. For the first time since they'd come into the room he steps round the chair to face the prisoner. 'Now, now, old son,' he says. 'Don't fret. Don't fret. Despite the seriousness of the ... er ... offence, nothing's ever so bad as something can't be done about it. Eh?' He gazes down at the prisoner with an approving look. 'Isn't that so, constable?' he asks, an almost tender expression on his face.

'Absolutely gospel,' replies the constable with contagious enthusiasm. He wants to handle it right. He hopes one day to become a Chief Superintendent. A little glow of hope and joy lights up the prisoner's face. A strange tingle of excitement runs through him. Perhaps they'd only been winding him up and now that they'd had their fun and seen how he'd taken it like a man are going to release him.

'Yes,' says the sergeant, resting his big backside on the table and staring down at the prisoner. 'Nothing that can't be sorted out.'

The man's eyes flit hopefully towards the sergeant's. Though he is squirming with anxiety to ask how, his position as a prisoner requires him to wait to be told.

The sergeant lets his body relax a little. 'Now, how can I explain it to you? The ... er ... difficult, overlapping, complicating aspects of police procedure, jurisprudence and case-swapping in terms you'll comprehend.'

The prisoner looks up, mouth agape, showing a few discoloured scattered teeth.

'Perhaps a cup of tea first might help?' says the constable, trying to enter into the spirit of the moment and jolly things along.

For reply the sergeant takes a sheet of paper from his tunic pocket. He is not about to be diverted by tea breaks. 'I want you to tell me one thing. Only one. If we drop the serious charge will you give us a plea on a bit of theft instead?' he asks, rattling the sheet of paper at the prisoner's head.

The prisoner hesitates a long time. The sergeant's new attitude has completely unnerved him. 'But I'm not guilty of any charge,' he counters at last.

The sergeant gives a deep sigh. 'There's a limit to the time I can spend coaxing prisoners and you have just passed that limit.' He takes a step towards the suspect, who, completely unnerved by now, grimly nods his head. The sergeant stops in mid stride. 'So we're being sensible at last? Now, who mentioned something about tea round here?' He smiles, turning to the constable.

He's utterly alone. There is no feeling of being in the right place or doing the right thing. The common is deserted. The cold wind blows round him in miserable gusts, making it difficult for the Limp to walk quickly enough to generate heat in his body. There is something that sets him apart. A look of having been rejected and isolated. For most lonely people identity does not exist. He has an intense longing to be near other humans, but since he came back from the Falklands everywhere seems changed and he hasn't fitted in . . . though he's tried.

'Enough.'

It's too cold. He walks quickly in the direction of the tube. As quickly as his feet will allow, that is. Around him, in the uncrowded street, people keep distance as if fearing touch. Always the same, thinks Limp, for those with a handicap.

In the lift, surrounded by people, Limp feels warmth and security pervading him. Later, waiting for the train, amid the crowds, this feeling becomes more intense, filling his mind, pushing out all previous negative emotions. Like a drug addict administering his first fix of the day he enters the packed train. Hours pass unnoticed as he journeys endlessly, like a child, dizzy and excited with free fairground rides.

Hours later, in the timelessness of the tunnel, the late-night revellers are thinning. As the warm bodies disperse, he sees his chances disappearing. But not his desire. On an impulse he leaves the train, unthinkingly ascending the escalator, taking in the pretty girls in various stages of undress. Advertisements of bras, slips, stockings. The girls seem to dazzle, with three-D effect. One looks over her shoulder, winking provocatively. Another puts out her tongue. Yet another peeps and beckons cheekily. Giddiness flooding over him, he reaches the top.

As he turns to fade into yet another tunnel the image

comes to life. A beautiful long-legged young woman approaches, abruptly turning into the station toilet. The Limp looks quickly around then follows her in. He glimpses the woman's back as she closes and bolts the cubicle door, unaware that she is not alone. Standing with his back against the outer door he makes a decision. Bending down he quickly wedges his stick under the door. Straightening up briskly, kicks back smartly with parade-ground precision, driving the stick home with a dull thud.

An apologetic voice floats out. 'Hello. Are you locking up? I shan't be a moment.'

Making no answer he crosses carefully to her door, but his shoes are noisy. He waits quietly. She flushes. He tenses. Her high heels clip the dark-tiled floor. The bolt slides. She stands there, holding the door slightly ajar. He makes a lunge for her but miscalculates, stumbling. She jumps back with a shriek, locking herself back in.

Limp throws his cap on top of a big metal toolbox standing in the corner by some wash-basins. He zips the bolt of an empty cubicle back and forth, noting its strength. He must gain entry before his dreadful pleasure gives way to slowly rising fear. Time is of the essence.

'Come on, sweetie. Open up. You can't stay in there all night,' he calls out chidingly, like a bold lover to a mischievous girlfriend.

She begins to stiffen with fear. 'What do you want? I've only got my ticket and a few pounds.'

'Come on. Don't be shy. I'm not the big bad wolf so don't force me to huff and puff and blow the door down.'

Limp whistles softly to himself. A drink wouldn't go to waste but the best he can do is a paper cup of water from the wash-basin. After a mouthful, he throws it back with a disgusted splash. Stalemate. How do these things turn out? No matter! If he could only get on with it.

'If you don't go away I shall scream.'

He's worried by this but calls her bluff. 'Yes, that *would* be nice. I'd like to hear you screaming. Go on. Just for me. No one else can hear anyway. They've all locked up and gone home.'

Silence.

'God, it's so hot. Will you let me have a drink of water, please?'

'I'm not stopping you. There's plenty in the tap. Come out and drink as much as you like.'

Her heels click. Is she coming out? No, she stays put.

He breaks the silence that suddenly descends. 'Suit yourself. I can wait. But you're going to get awfully thirsty.'

Both prisoners together, he wonders what the time is.

Summoning up her courage the woman asks, 'Why are you interested in me?'

'I have a reason.'

'What reason? Please, I don't know you and I'm sure you don't know me. Do you?'

'I know your sisters.'

'You must be mistaken. I have no sisters.'

He laughs drily. 'Oh, but you have. Many, many sisters.'

'Well, where did you see these . . . my sisters? What did they say?' she asks coaxingly.

He notices she's taking a different tack. 'Oh, I haven't actually had the pleasure of speaking to them yet. I've only seen their pictures.'

'Pictures?' She's puzzled. 'Where?'

'Everywhere. On the street, in the cinema, on the telly, in the magazines, papers, books, even the tube. Yes, especially the dear old tube.'

'Adverts! That's some sort of crazy fantasy. You should be ashamed of yourself.'

'Quite so. Quite so. And who creates it? Eh? When it gets to fantasy and far beyond, it's time to pull in your boobs or take the consequences. But do I despise you? No. The real tyrant is in your absurd sex confidence which doesn't allow you to consider what you are doing – even now.'

'Oh my God, this is so stupid. Why me?'

'Why is metal drawn to a magnet?'

Stupid. Of course it is. Wading through a sea of covert

sex. Professionally dishevelled clothing. Slits to the right, left, up the back, up the front. Did I glimpse an undergarment there? Stockings or tights? Shaking that mane till it's all tousled. Preening. Or maybe just teasing.

Limp glimpses his scarred face in the wash-stand mirror. Yes, I must be stupid, he thinks. Throw away my liberty for five minutes' pleasure. Or anxiety?

The woman's fingers pluck at her dress freeing it from the inner parts of her thighs. 'God, this is ridiculous. I'm so hot.'

'Exactly how I feel too. Do you know how you make the boys sweat?'

'Do you have to be so crude?'

'I'm just verbalising my stress.'

'God, what are you? Some kind of psychopath?'

'Psychopath is a very loose term, sweetie,' he rebukes her. What's being said is not being heard.

Trying to satisfy desire's like throwing fat on a fire to put it out. Limp stands staring at the door.

'Won't you tell me your name?' He waits. 'Well, at least what you work at. Are you working? . . . No? Perhaps you're fabulously rich. Dressed like that I'd say you were an extra in a Dallas film.'

'I'm a secretary.'

'Oh, I shall call you Miss Tippex then as you seem to have made some mistake tonight.' He chuckles bitterly.

There is a long silence. Limp wonders what she's doing in there. Standing? Leaning? Sitting? Clever girl. Less tiresome. More functionally appropriate too. So near but yet so far. Still time to cut and run. And he might have done, except her voice comes through the door again.

'Have you got a problem or something?' she asks boldly.

'I've got quite a few,' says Limp, 'but I haven't got time to discuss them with you now.'

After this exchange there is a long silence, broken eventually by the woman.

'Please, let me have a drink of water. You can pass it under the door.' This is said matter-of-factly, naturally.

She doesn't want to plead when he might even get a little more pleasure from the struggle.

Limp, relenting, whistles softly to himself as he fills a cup and proffers it at the gap where he glimpses her ankles. Her hand grasps the cup. His hand grasps her bag. She wobbles back on her haunches, shrieking with surprise.

'Sorry. But since you seem to be in no hurry to come out . . .'

'Please,' she says, still startled by her loss, 'you can keep the money. Just let me have my letters back.'

'All in good time, all in good time . . .'

After that little burst of excitement he settles down. Already rummaging in the bag he walks over to sit on the toolbox, takes out her compact with mirror attached and holds it up. Looking at it with contempt, he slams it back under the door with a clatter, hissing, 'Yes, always pretty. Any time, any place, anywhere.'

She sits, riding the toilet bowl, unnaturally aware of the sound of his voice.

The mirror, slithering along the floor, bounces off the door jamb, smashing into pieces.

Limp continues sifting through the contents of the bag. A large felt-tipped marking pen takes his eye. He holds it up, looking at it quizzically. 'Well, Miss Tippex. Surely you're not a graffiti artist? Do demon authors ply their art in women's toilets? Can it be true Kilroy's been here? Or is it his missus who visits this loo?' The pen follows the compact under the door.

He takes out her purse. 'Ah, the root of all evil, so they say. I don't believe a word of it.' He returns the purse unopened to the bag as her letters take his interest.

He begins speaking as he leafs through them. 'The more one knows about a person the better. Don't you think? Gives a relationship a more solid basis. Wouldn't you agree? We may even find we have quite a few interests in common.'

She does not reply, pulling her feet slowly up against the base of the china bowl.

Limp's exhilarated. He finally selects one. He doesn't get to read many letters like this.

Settling back on the box he reads aloud: ' "Hi, Julie. Thank you for such a lovely weekend. Your parents are nice." Oh, it's Julie, is it? And you've got nice parents too. Do you think they'd like to meet me?' He laughs hollowly. ' "They must have worked so hard to cater for us all. It was really enjoyable. I must have you all up to our place when Daddy comes back from the States." Oh, it's Daddy, is it? "Well, I'm simply bursting to tell you about this guy I met at Mandy's twenty-first. Fab. Rich. Drives a Lamborghini – or should I say flies it? Got a smart little flat in Hampstead and a cottage in the country." That's nice. Makes a change from sleeping in a cardboard box. "Can't wait to meet him again." I'll bet you can't! "All the girls were fluttering around him at Mandy's. So I've got all my fingers crossed that he doesn't forget about me. Well, I'd better close for now, Julie. Old Tobias has just looked in for the third time. Better look busy. See you . . ." ' Limp's voice tapers off.

He drops the bag. It has suddenly lost all interest. He cocks his head. He can't be sure. Was that a noise outside? Moving towards the door, he bends to retrieve his stick, then cautiously eases his head round the door, only to pull it back sharply. Fear showing on his face, he looks round for some other way out of this hygienic cul-de-sac. But he's trapped. Boxed in. Resignedly he glances round again. Boxed in. Of course! He lifts the lid of the toolbox, knocking his cap to one side as he scrambles in. He has no sooner lowered the lid when the door flies open.

The big sergeant enters, running his eyes around the place, whistling softly to himself as he spots the bag.

Could turn out to be a profitable night after all, he thinks, opening it, deftly pocketing the purse without a second thought. Then, giving one final glance around, he leaves.

'Everything OK?' asks the constable, who's been checking elsewhere when they meet up outside.

'Yeah.'

'Same here. What you got there?'

'Bit of lost property.'

'Any money in it?'

'No. Nothing,' says the sergeant as they continue dutifully on their rounds.

The silence that follows in the white-tiled brightness of the ladies' loo is finally shattered by metallic rattlings, muffled cries.

'Miss. Can you hear me?'

The clasp has dropped into place, securing the lid of the box. What a turn up.

She listens doubtingly as the voice grows louder.

'Please. Get me out of here.'

Wary now of conversation and annoyed by his apparent teasing plea she snaps grimly. 'Don't waste your time making such a racket. I'm not about to fall for any more of your tricks.'

'No, no. It's not a trick. I'm locked inside this bloody toolbox. Come and see for yourself.' He rattles the lid. 'Please. I meant you no harm. Now I'm stuck. Just come and see for yourself how stuck I am.' The rattling of the lid increases.

The woman sits on the toilet seat, holding her head between her hands, remembering despairingly how ridiculously careful she was when crossing a street. She stares absently at her strained pale face, white as the underside of the basin bowls reflected in another segment of the broken mirror. The sudden rattle of the box's lid startles her anew, but the idea has taken hold. She bends to investigate.

Crouching down she picks up a piece of the broken compact mirror, angling it under the bottom of the door. Slowly she pans the room. Her heart gives a leap when the mirror, focusing on the box, reveals the fallen clasp.

'Please, dear. I won't harm you. Just get me out of here.' Limp's weak vocal plea reaches her once more.

Seized by a thrilling hope, she begins collecting her scattered belongings and gingerly opens the door. Cautiously she approaches the box. The silence grows as seconds pass.

'Hurry up, dear, before I suffocate.'

She gives an involuntary start at the seemingly unreal

voice coming from the box. Consternation and indecision cross her face.

'What's wrong? Is it too heavy? Can you manage? Are you still there?' Desperately Limp bangs, his breath coming in short painful gasps because of his damaged lung.

She begins straightening her clothes and shaking out her hair. She stares down at the box with uncomfortable doubt. Then moves briskly towards the door. But the continual frantic rattling of the box's lid causes her to stop. Turning thoughtfully she walks back and, picking up the cap that has fallen to one side of the box, places it on top. Then she walks out into the locked station.

L eading a cute but nervous-looking little chihuahua, a pretty young woman enters the train wearing a white blouse and a short black skirt that shows her exact shape. She makes her way towards the only available seat, half-way along the carriage. An expensively dressed good-looking man sitting opposite, bronzed face and dark sunglasses, never averts his gaze as her foot, becoming entangled in the dog's lead, causes her to miss her footing. Teetering on the tips of her high heels she flops backwards inelegantly on to the seat, her skirt riding up her thighs. Though the man never glances directly at her, she feels slightly irritated that her legs seem to be occupying the attention that would otherwise have been levelled at the dog. As the man continues to stare, she begins fiddling with the large bag she holds in her lap, carefully turning it this way and that until it dangles over her knees. Satisfied now that no one can peep up her dress, she sits back square and rigid. When the train reaches the next stop, the man rises, grasping the strap hanger with one hand. Leaning over her, he dips into his inside pocket with the other. The dog looks up expectantly as he pulls something out which, after a couple of clicks, unfolds into a long white cane. Straightening, he taps his way to the door.

Since giving up the drink Mo has been getting pains in his head and back. Some days it is so bad he has to lie down flat on the floor to ease it. This finally forces him to consult a doctor, who after leisurely diagnosing some symptoms in Latin and promptly prescribing some blue pills in English, hands Mo a chit for the chemist. The blue pills have no effect and Mo returns to the doctor who prescribes some larger green pills. But as the green pills have the same effect as the blue pills Mo is forced to return yet again to the surgery, whereupon the doctor advises taking the blues with the greens, before and after meals.

A week passes, then two, with no positive result, except that Mo's back becomes worse. Wearily he returns again to face the doctor who is puzzled. In all his experience he cannot recall a single instance of a patient ever being able to remain *compos mentis* after a course of his little blues – never mind remembering where the surgery is or recall the original complaint. Yet here is this one, bold as you please, whingeing on about his back again. And this after a double dose of little blues and larger greens. Obviously a problem case, but he knows where to send problem cases. The time wasters. Patients who persist stubbornly with their symptoms. Refusers to respond.

'Take this phone number, and give them a ring,' he says, flicking a piece of paper in the general direction of Mo.

'Thank you, doctor, but who are they?' Mo asks, picking the paper up from where it has landed on the floor. The doctor gives him a withering look. This patient's habit of asking questions is annoying. With such an appalling record for drinking perhaps he might fall under a bus.

'Aromatherapist, my good man. Aromatherapist. Now you just pop along and send the next person in. There's a good chap.

'Aromatherapist . . .' he muses, as Mo leaves the room. 'There's an imposing name for a gang of pagan chancers.'

Mo makes his way towards the aromatherapist's house. He hadn't wanted to make an appointment but the pain in his back has got worse since his last visit to the doctor, and this has forced him to phone. The woman who answers tells him her name is Nadia, and that she practises a new form of alternative medicine. Her friendly, confident air, encourages Mo to give it a try. Nadia lives in the bottom two floors of an old Victorian house. The flat contains eight large rooms of which two have been converted into a clinic with its own private entrance. It was once a very rich and fashionable area of North London, but, along with clothes, housing fashions have changed and when the price was low enough Nadia and her socially conscious friends nipped smartly in, buying up flats and houses before the local council gathered the wherewithal to do likewise for the borough's homeless.

Mo walks up the path at the side of the house and knocks respectfully. The door is answered by a tall, attractive woman.

'Nadia?' says Mo.

'Yes, I am, and you're Mo, aren't you? Please, come in,' she replies, with a pleasant enough expression, turning slowly, head up, back straight, leaving Mo to close the door and follow.

As the door opens directly into the waiting room he does not have far to go. It is a very clean room, white walls and ceiling making it appear extra bright.

Two paintings hang opposite each other. On a sign suspended between them Mo reads, 'You're starting to progress in therapy when your former anxiety becomes panic.' Nadia beckons Mo to be seated. All her movements seem unhurried as she lowers herself down close beside him on the sofa. Much like a girlfriend, or, if not a girlfriend, then at least a concerned favourite sister. Mo answers her questions politely, never offering information, yet never holding anything back. In place of his work telephone number she asks him his star sign. Instead of demanding a medical number she gently enquires of his previous night's sleep. She does not make him feel that he is lying, nor that he might be wasting her time.

'You see,' she says, when she has finished asking him about his back, 'by its fruit the tree is known. By its stem the flower grown. But in your case the stem has become slightly crushed. Oh, nothing that cannot be put right,' she adds hastily, in response to Mo's worried frown. 'But it will take time.'

'How much time?' asks Mo, glancing hopefully at the walls for a clock.

'Well, one can never give exact dates in these circumstances, but in your case, given that the tension is deeply rooted, I'd say about six months.'

'Six months?' repeats Mo.

'Yes. Your life up to now seems to have been set a pace that it cannot live with.'

It has, that, thinks Mo. Well, he's often done six months in far worse company than this woman's promises to be. She looks directly at him with a warm friendly smile, or is it the professionally induced friendship of a shopkeeper before a sale?

'May I ask what the treatment consists of?' enquires Mo politely.

'You may indeed. Look at it as a rebirthing,' she says mystically. 'A rebirthing through the nose rather than the soul. A sort of psychic bypass surgery if you like.' After a pause she goes over to a small table by the door, picks up a diary and starts leafing through it, while Mo sits weighing her up. 'OK? Let's make an appointment. I can fit you in at 7 p.m. on Wednesday,' she says, inclining her head at Mo.

'Yes, that will do nicely,' he answers deferentially, rising to join her at the table.

Her next words strike Mo dumb. 'Would you like to pay by cheque or Access?' When Mo does not reply, she hastens to add, 'Of course cash is fine. It's £10 a session.'

Like a boxer who's taken too much leather to the head, Mo shakes his in bewilderment. 'I thought it was free. You know, like on the National Health. If I'd have known it cost money I wouldn't have come,' he says, trying to catch her eye. But Nadia, biting her lip, is carefully avoiding meeting Mo's eyes, standing there in her long dress with its tight bodice, lost in thought at this detail she has overlooked.

A sixties throwback, earth mother, thinks Mo, although Nadia could not be more than thirty-five.

'I see,' she says at last, 'you're unemployed, are you?'

'Yes,' he says, and seeing that she looks a bit crestfallen, adds hastily, 'I'm sorry if I wasted your time.'

'Oh, don't worry about that,' she says, slowly lifting her eyes now to look at him. 'I worked for a firm that went bankrupt once. Perhaps you could so something for me in exchange for your treatment?'

Mo smiles inwardly, as his mind rapidly runs through all the various possibilities, then plumps for being a gardener, rightly judging that well-spoken earth mothers usually like the soil.

'That's splendid,' says Nadia, hardly believing her luck. 'I've got some work that needs doing in my garden.' Her apparently open, honest way of speaking seems to unnerve Mo.

'I'll do it . . .' he falters, 'but I can't do anything fancy. I just cut grass, dig over, rough stuff . . . that sort of thing, you know.'

She certainly does know, for like most women with fairly large gardens she's had varied experiences of the differing types of horticultural experts one meets from season to season. Still, if only he can cut grass. If he can do just that . . . thinks Nadia hopefully. She has a passion for gardens, which simmers down considerably when it comes actually to gardening. She does want to get the place into shape, though, and this man might just be different. He doesn't seem like a drunk, a drug addict or a con man.

'Oh, there's no fancy work,' she confides. 'Just a bit of lawn mowing. Lawn,' she repeats, laughing engagingly. 'It's a field.' This is said with such a sincere girl-next-door smile she nearly has Mo offering to do the job for nothing. 'I just need someone to cut the grass.' Of course, now that the ice has been broken it is also possible to mention fallen trees, heaps of rotting rubbish, sheds that need clearing out. That is before one can actually get down to cutting a blade of grass. But that all sounds heavy work and heavy work should cost lots of money. However, instead Nadia offers Mo free treatment to counteract the effects of any extra stress that might ensue during the course of his labours.

'It'll take quite a time,' she says. 'If you're not working you can come as often as you like.' Mo readily agrees, promising to call again and start work the next day.

Mo gets off the tube. As he walks the length of the platform towards the exit from the Piccadilly Line the train passes him out. Wheels rattling and clattering, amid a spray of sparks. Meeting up with Nadia has been a stroke of luck, thinks Mo, but really he still doesn't know how he is going to continue to keep himself together financially. However, the thought that he is now on his way to a legitimate job gives him a warm, secure feeling. He even got up extra early to make himself some sandwiches for his dinner.

He's still romancing about the job when Nose Job lurches up out of nowhere, shouting a greeting, indicating with his head two more of the lads lying on a platform seat. Needless to say they're all in a bad way from drink – and needing more. They don't have to put the bite too deeply. Mo always gives with a good heart, remembering all those mornings when he'd woken with his vision blurred, tongue furred and speech slurred. After leaving them the price of a bottle he continues on his way.

It is with his new worker's eye that he notices the platform has not been swept. A hollow in the wall looks out of place too. Like something's missing from it, he thinks vaguely. A fire extinguisher? A bucket of sand, perhaps? Even a first-aid box? In reality, it had once housed a cigarette-vending machine but since the law

79

against smoking was passed making it surplus to requirements it has been removed. Its place is soon to be filled, however, for London Regional Transport, ever mindful of its more robust passengers' physical needs and not wishing to spoil its more arty types' sense of aesthetics either, intends to fill the ugly gap with a smart new condom dispenser. Of course, Mo can't know all this, and thinks only that LRT are lax. Tut, tut, tut.

A couple of well-equipped buskers are just starting up their continual paid rehearsal as the train pulls in with throbbing grunts which idle down to soothing murmurs as its doors hiss open. Mo weaves his way on board among the other passengers.

The train journeys on, picking up and depositing numerous office workers of both sexes at various exits. And then it's Mo's turn to get off and make for his exit. In the absence of a ticket collector, he and a handful of other passengers pass quickly through the barrier. Out on the street at last, Mo makes his way towards Nadia's house.

Today, instead of going to the side entrance he goes to the front door, feeling a sense of elation as he waits. The secure, carefree feeling of doing something for a friend. She opens the door to his knock, dressed in jeans and a man's jacket. It gives her a presence she seems to lack in the clinic. Mo feels awkward now, and tries hard not to show it. The other night he might have put out his hand and touched her. Even given her a little cuddle, but he wouldn't try it now though. Today she's as far away from him as a countess in her castle.

'Hello, Mo,' she greets him strongly, with no sign of remembered embarrassment as Mo smiles back lopsidedly to hide his missing teeth. A big strong healthy-looking lad of about fourteen suddenly appears behind Nadia who, sensing his presence, automatically squeezes to one side. Then, without being aware of it, she puts out a restraining hand, halting the boy for a split second.

'Where are your manners, Hadrian?' (A certain show for

Mo is unmistakable in her action.) 'Don't just push past when I'm speaking to someone.'

The boy does not appear fazed by the rebuke and, shrugging off her arm, continues on his way so that she is forced to call out after him. 'Would you mind telling me where you are off to, Hadrian?'

'Justin's,' slings back the boy.

'Have you finished all your homework?' Hadrian does not seem to hear this and she has to shout even louder. 'Well, don't be too late back.'

She turns to face Mo. 'My son Hadrian. Never a dull moment round here.'

If Mo is disappointed that she does not live alone he never shows it, replying, 'Well, I'm ready to start.'

She stands aside to let him come in. 'Good, there's plenty to do,' she answers, looking at his out-of-date clothes. Her female Persian, who is doing likewise, suddenly stiffens at the sight of Mo's scuffed grey trainers peeping out from under his bell bottoms. Taking them for two bedraggled alley cats, she disappears behind the armchair, in a flurry of fluff. 'Do you want a cup of tea before you start?' she asks, in a way that is both lighthearted yet businesslike.

'Yes, please,' says Mo, knowing that she might only have asked out of politeness, never expecting him to accept. But then she isn't the sort of person you could get to know in an hour or so, and Mo hopes that the tea will break the ice.

She stares out of the french windows as she waits for the kettle to boil. The windows open on to a vast, neglected expanse of grass. A necessary neglect, she tells herself, while she built up her healing practice. It had once been nice, though, and with this man's help could be so again.

Mo gazes round with interest at the pine kitchen units which match the wooden floor. A painting here and there takes the bareness off the walls. The middle of the room is taken up by a large wooden table, surrounded by wooden chairs. Against a far wall stands a worn leather sofa, while two matching armchairs pressed up against one another force the telly into a corner. Everything seems made of natural materials, including the large ornamental fire surround and a valuable decorated antique cupboard. With so much crushed into it the room appears far smaller than it actually is.

Nadia's voice interrupts his furniture-gazing. 'It's got cold earlier this year,' she says, giving an involuntary shudder. 'I'm afraid autumn's nearly here.'

'Yes,' says Mo, his lips twisting with humour, 'the pigeons have started to cough.'

She smiles to herself before turning to look at him with a frown, perhaps an unconscious reminder that he's come there to work.

Mo sits silently, waiting for the tea. He doesn't want to talk about the weather and doesn't know what more to say. He is beginning to regret having asked for the tea now, wishing he was out in the garden where he feels he would be more at ease. He rises to tell her he's going to start without waiting for the tea when she calls out, as if antici-pating his move, 'The loo is through there.'

Mo looks at the door she has indicated and, not wishing to add insult to injury if she presumed mind-reading powers, decides to use it. He comes back to find Nadia sitting at the table pouring out the tea. She smiles up at him without speaking. The feeling of comfort he'd felt at first with her and the room, returns. He sits down, more relaxed.

After passing Mo a mug of tea, she picks up a letter from the table, nodding at him. 'Excuse me, I just want to finish reading this. It's from one of my clients abroad.' Mo smiles at her, and without a word takes a sip from his mug, which nearly scalds him. This provokes immediate action. He begins blowing, but as the tea is so hot, gentle puffs will not suffice and he is soon forced to resort to loud, vigorous blasts.

Nadia tolerates this interruption to her reading with no more than an occasional, tight-lipped, sidelong glance. (Her patience with those who lack etiquette is obviously boundless.) The tick of a large clock on the wall is the only other sound in the room, and seems to be synchronised with Mo's blowing. Who knows how long Mo might have continued, if one of his gusts had not caused a paper to slide off the table and float to the floor, giving Nadia the chance to intervene? 'My goodness,' she exclaims. 'What a whirlwind. Breathing out is in direct opposition to aromatherapy and may spoil any benefits that may accrue.' The gale ceases as Mo looks up at her from his tea. 'We must train ourselves to be conscious only of the incoming breath, which brings benefits undreamed of in the form of invigorating, deliberately chosen, life-enhancing smells.'

'Sniffing is preferable to snorting then?' says Mo.

'How quaint.' She smiles patronisingly. 'You've termed it more tersely but seem to have grasped the essence of it.' Then, more firmly, she adds, 'Well done!' And, as if infused with energy from Mo's understanding, she jumps up, grasps the two mugs and goes over to the sink. With forced enthusiasm she shouts back over her shoulder, 'If you have as much a grasp of horticulture as you seem to have for aromatherapy, oh, what a garden we shall eventually have.' Mo grins and, taking the hint, makes for the glass doors.

Mo works hard and patiently. Sifting foliage, sorting fallen trees, separating bushes that have bunched together in thick entwined masses.

Nadia watches him from the window. Either he has no understanding of the work involved, or he's forgotten that he only agreed to cut grass, she thinks.

She'd expected him to challenge her about the extra work, having anticipated some sharp bargaining. Surprised to find herself dwelling on the subject she immediately curbs the impulse, telling herself that this man obviously has a low value of himself. Different perception. Not very sensitive. The guy looks dependable though and is obviously a good worker. After this she thinks about it no more and sits down to finish the article she's preparing for the *Borough Boundaries* health column, which she writes every two weeks. This week's article pertains to the unfair health treatment ethnics have received over the years at the hands of the white ruling classes. A subject dear to her heart.

Of course Mo *has* noticed, and been disappointed at

first, that the job was not the straightforward gardening she'd led him to believe. He makes for the back door to speak to her about it, then stops, as if unable to decide how to approach her, consoling himself instead with the idea as he returns to work that after the debris has been cleared he will be left with the comparatively easier, and hopefully regular, gardening job. There is, after all, no other way of looking at it, given his record, if he wants work. 'No gain without pain,' as the gym instructor said to the weightlifter. And it's true as Mo finds out when he continues with an axe, a saw and a will. First slicing the branches from the trees that he's sorted, then sawing the trunks and thicker branches into logs and stacking them in neat piles against the broken fence at the bottom of the garden. Time passes or stands still: Mo doesn't notice as the work taxes his strength and keeps him under a heavy strain. It is late in the evening and already dark when he finishes and leaves for home.

Mo stands in the clinic's doorway watching Nadia who is describing large circles in the air with a small twig in her hand. Her eyes give an indefinable smile when they meet Mo's, as if he's caught her in the midst of some embarrassing act.

'To clear the place of bad vibes,' she says, stopping her wand waving with a satisfied nod which seems to imply that no bad karma lingers now. On a small table specially set out for the purpose stand half a dozen medium-sized bottles of different coloured liquids. She beckons Mo to an armchair, its cover patterned with olde-worlde cottages surrounded with wild flowers. A long bench with a mattress on it stands by a far wall, taking up most of the room. Slotted into holders all around the walls are little posies of plastic flowers.

'Among a host of other ailments, most of my clients suffer from hay fever too,' she begins, after noticing Mo eyeing them, 'which the pollen in real flowers would only aggravate.'

'Yes, but they'd drum up more business,' chirps Mo.

She gives him a penetrating stare. Mo, feeling he should not have referred to money, looks down at his worn trainers, promising to buy himself a strong pair of boots one day when he gets a proper job or finds a publisher – if he lasts that long.

Feeling that she has asserted herself sufficiently, Nadia starts to busy herself at the table. From the noise, and a quick under-eyed glance, Mo sees that she is tipping a measure of liquid from each bottle on to several of the plastic flowers taken at random from the wall.

'Would you mind blowing your nose before we start your first treatment, Mo?' she asks, giving him a box of Kleenex and a friendly smile. 'Clean nostrils are an essential element on the royal road to aromatherapeutic bliss.' His loud blowing causes Mo to miss the bit about the bliss. 'There, isn't that better? Think of all the gunge that must have cleared away,' she says as Mo, soiled Kleenex in hand, makes a few respectful attempts to locate some means of disposal before ramming it into his pocket.

'Good,' says Nadia, passing three of the flowers back and forth in front of Mo's face, before placing them on the table. 'Can you smell that beautiful essence of cow daisy and tulip?' she asks, raising her eyes with fluttering delicacy towards the ceiling, leaving Mo impatient with hopes of the bliss that is to come.

'Yes.'

'Fine,' she says, shifting the three flowers about on the table with the dexterity of an Oxford Street spiv shuffling his cards. 'Only one of these flowers contains scent. I want you to close your eyes and by smell alone tell me which one it is.'

Mo bends forward over the table, eyes tightly clenched. 'It's just like Find the Lady,' he says enthusiastically, with an outward show of deep deliberation, sniffing like a bloodhound. All the flowers smell the same to him, but as he is enjoying the game, and also to please her, he continues. He has to wait longer than he expected, but at last he thinks he's picked up the scent.

'This is the one,' he shouts eagerly, clutching one of the flowers, which on opening his eyes he finds to be a twig. It looks remarkably like the one with which she has consecrated the room.

They look at each other, Mo holding the twig in his hand laughing; a schoolboy caught in the act by his teacher. She leans forward, black hair cascading, accentuating the whiteness of her skin in her low-cut blouse.

'You're like a child looking for praise. Your immediate reaction was to win,' she says crossly, taking the twig from Mo's hand. Mo is seduced into silence, not so much by her words, which are tinged with contempt, as by the tiny golden freckle nestling alone between the swell of her breasts. Somehow he wishes the treatment involved touching. He would have liked to get up and give her a kiss but, looking at a notice on the wall, he forces the thought from his mind. 'The first lesson is that a lesson can be dangerous,' it reads, 'but if you would smell the aroma of the spheres, stop breathing' (Lady Victoria Sniffstreet, First Grand Mistress of Aromatherapy, 1771).

Nadia's voice brings him back to the real world. 'You must concentrate on the smell, otherwise the treatment is useless. At the moment you are a beginner, but take heart, the beginner and the expert are both alike.'

After a while she says, 'Now shall we just lie back,' pressing him gently down on to the mattress by his shoulders. Mo enjoys it when she says 'we', as if whatever is to happen to him from now on she is to share in.

The iron-featured police sergeant's hand is shaking. Shaking the dice. He needs a seven to get out of jail. They land six up, shit out, no good.

'Unlucky, sarge,' says the new recruit.

Fucking rookies. All the same. Healthy-faced bastards. Hair stiff and virile, cropped close to the bone. Solid bone between the two ears, thinks the sergeant. But lucky, oh, yes. Youth will be served. Well, he'd soon see how well youth served when the footballers landed from Scotland. Up to now he's only had to deal with a few broken-toothed, broken-homed, broken-minded dossers. Yes, next May would separate the men from the boys.

Down below the Transport Police office, the station has started to fill up. The preacher comes in out of the cold, pushing his stooge in a wheelchair. The preacher's about six foot, heavy-built, dressed all in black. Except for a white shirt. He wears a large-brimmed hat like a Quaker. His stooge is an old man, yellow skin drawn tight across prominent cheekbones. His watery, soulless eyes stare straight ahead. Both live in the local dosshouse.

The preacher goes into his spiel. 'According to the words of the prophet, God shall not be mocked. This man was saved in 1985,' he leans in, whispering out of the side of his mouth. 'Get up, say a few words.'

The old boy makes a few attempts to rise, gets lucky on the third. Staggers forward, speaking, lips moving, nothing coming out. The big 'un clasps his protégé round the shoulders, guides him back to the chair. He's got enough troubles without the chosen one forgetting his lines.

Talking, covering up. 'Yes, brothers and sisters, this is one leper that came back, and I tell ye there shall be more rejoicing in heaven over one sinner that returns than all the ninety-nine that are saved.' He pushes the old boy down into the chair. 'Yes, the miracle of Lourdes tells us . . .'

The old boy becomes gripped by a furious bout of coughing. Dredging up a lump of phlegm, he slides over sideways as he spits it on to the floor. The preacher grabs him by the lapels, straightens him up. The greatest miracle is how he's still fucking alive in that condition.

Finn is watching four blacks sitting on the station's white-tiled wall like jays on a fence. Silent ghetto-blasters look suspect devices in their supple-fingered hands. Smartly dressed office girl saunters by. Handbag swinging at her side. The boys drop loose-boned to the floor, bounce around in trainers with that bobbing walk. The bag's got a secure strap and buckle. One of the blacks gives her a jostle.

'Watch out, Leroy, it ain't no toy.'

The sergeant can hear the hum and bustle of the station, and feel its flow. Like a doctor taking a pulse. And right now that pulse does not feel normal. It seems to convey more beggars than passengers on the station today. He stares at the Government grey wall.

'Time for a little tour of duty, constable. Make sure the equilibrium's not disturbed. Keep the status quo.'

'Right, sarge,' says the rookie, putting away the Monopoly board. 'Where shall we start?'

'Bit of dosser-culling. Don't forget your gloves.' The sergeant was the first to see the possibilities, for hygienic reasons, of using dish-washing gloves when manhandling dossers. (Had an article about it published in the *Police Gazette*.)

Leroy's trying to open the bag as the sergeant hits the station.

'You got a ticket, boy?' The voice makes Leroy jump.

'Sure, man.'

'Where're you going?'

'Brixton.'

The sergeant runs his eyes over the four of them. 'Don't miss that tube or we'll take a little walk when I get back.'

Alvin's getting set for a quick withdrawal. 'Let's go, Leroy.'

'Sam, you frightened of that rass-cloth?'

'Come off it, Blood Clot. You hear that mother speaking to me?'

'Aw shit, man, let's go.'

'OK, Alvin, you's right.'

'Right on, man!' drifts back in broken echoes from the Victoria Line.

As they continue on their rounds the constable asks, 'You think they was up to anything, sarge?'

'Oh, yes. They're at it, all right. But you've got to catch them bang to rights because of Clause 8.'

The constable blinks. 'Clause 8, sarge?'

'Yep. That's the one,' says the sergeant. 'Don't ever get yourself impaled on that one. Middle-class whites, ethnic circle guilt law. Best to be on the safe side. Anyway, not having acquired education, money or property at the expense of our Commonwealth cousins – unlike others who shall be nameless – I don't fall down with guilt every time I look at a black.'

What a time to throw a wobbler. The old boy's gone blue in the face. Frothing at the mouth. Hands waving like a windmill. Knocks the preacher's hat off as he tries to subdue him. But his body's gone into jerking spasms, making an awful racket in the metal chair. The preacher sighs. He's going to have to find a new protégé soon to help Jesus with his PR.

Finn jumps in, taking advantage of the confusion, to make a collection with the hat. The good Lord helps those who help themselves, according to the words of the prophet.

Spring dew still glitters on the grass as Mo walks through the park on his way to the station. Outside the amusement arcade (still closed) as he crosses the central concourse, small boys and girls — all on the trot from the children's home — sit or stand against walls. Eyeing every well-dressed adult, they indulge the orphan's dream, destined to become tomorrow's meat, whores, next year's rent boys. Meantime, they wait to play the pinball machine.

As the tube rattles on, Mo realises how much he's missed Nadia, her garden and her household during the enforced lull from work throughout the worst of winter's fury. His back has begun to feel more comfortable too. The funny thing about it is it has only been since he ceased to expect anything from it that the flower power began to work.

The train jerks, braking, as it approaches his stop, its compartments rattling and bouncing over the joints, throwing passengers standing near the doors off balance so that they sway up against one another, first this way then that.

Alighting, Mo walks along in the subdued neon glow and stale humid air. In his pocket he feels for his newly purchased tube pass which is sitting comfortably on top of his packet of sandwiches. Both signal that he is back working again with a routine about to be re-established out of the muddle of his life. Without being able to read it, Mo recognises the notice from a distance. Knowing what it means, he turns on his heel and walks back along the solitary platform, cursing under his breath at being forced to climb the old, dimly lit metal emergency stairs. The only way to get back to the rest of the world.

They seem to go on for ever, twisting their way round the thick metal column. Like the stairs over at south London where boys await lone climbers, concealed in the alcoves. Mo begins to climb slowly, ever so slowly, one step at a time. He isn't expecting to meet anyone, but, then, no one usually is. Still, out of habit, he does not want to be out of breath, thus handing himself fatigued to a well-rested attacker. Eventually Mo emerges at the top with no worse attack than a stitch in his side.

He reaches Nadia's house with plenty of time to spare. Now that he has broken the back of the roughest work and regained some kind of order the real gardening can begin.

The door is opened by Hadrian. 'Oh, it's you,' he says petulantly, in a childish mood, abandoning Mo to close the door.

He's not very pleasant today, thinks Mo, and if he'd dared to think about it any deeper, might have added that no kids are very pleasant any day. But then he excuses them by allowing that they're still at school, after all. School kids or not, like their parents, when they choose to can still subject gardeners to severe social maulings. As he is closing the door Mo can hear raised voices yelling and screaming, coming from the living room. He soon discovers the cause on entering the room. Seated at a table, crouched over a chessboard, two of Hadrian's friends, urged on by two other boys, are arguing the merits and demerits of a move. Mo's 'hello' as he proceeds to put on the kettle is greeted by five disinterested grunts. Like teenagers everywhere, they argue and shout, but somehow those privately educated seem to shout louder and in more precise ways.

Watching the boys crowding round the chessboard as he brews the tea reminds Mo of the chess scene he frequented when he'd first come out of prison. It evokes memories of those coffee-house spectators who took delight in the skill (or lack of it) displayed by the players, and who also argued over the merits of moves. Kibitzers who claimed to see better, or at least as good a move as those chosen by the competing opponents, but who are not experiencing the game from the viewpoint of those engaged. For those actually playing things are different. In a chess match victory or defeat can hang on a thread. A few seconds behind on the clock, a momentary hesitation, a mistake in judgement, a mistimed blow on the flank, a sudden breakthrough in the centre — all can cost the game. Small things — but defeat waits on such and defeat is always waiting.

Out of politeness, Mo asks if anyone wants tea, knowing beforehand that the health-conscious lads only drink fruit juice or Perrier. He feels on common ground with them, looking down at the game.

'What shall I move?' asks the boy playing the black pieces of no one in particular.

Everyone answers simultaneously, 'Play the knight, Paul.'

'Move your bishop.'

'Try castling.'

'Seize the centre.'

Mo joins the ranks of the kibitzers. 'When you don't know what to do, wait for your opponent to make the play. It's sure to be wrong.'

At first they pay him no heed, looking silently from one to the other, but Mo holds his ground, staring at the board.

'Can he play chess?' asks Paul, with a scornful look towards Hadrian.

'Apparently,' replies Hadrian dourly.

At this Paul bangs down his knight with an arrogant twist of the wrist, capturing his opponent's useless doubled pawn. A caveman's move.

Had they begun to argue with him or even in youthful high spirits to have pulled faces behind his back, he would not have felt so out of place as he does now. But to see them assume the austere and disdainfully commanding attitudes of their parents so suddenly — and naturally — seems somehow unnatural. Leaving them to it Mo goes over to the cooker and pours himself a cup of tea. About to dispose of the empty tea-bag he notices that the rubbish bin is stuffed to overflowing. He looks over at the preoccupied youths before carefully gathering the top of the plastic liner together, so as not to spill any of its contents, and carries it outside to the dustbin – computer games, high-tech gadgets, videos, bikes, word processors . . . glutted with distractions, is it any wonder Hadrian regularly forgets to take the refuse out, clear his leavings after meals or generally help around the house? But since Mo has been encouraged to believe that he is part of the household, what objection can there possibly be to him undertaking little household chores?

Mo reflects as he sits watching Nadia walk across the clinic to greet him, what a pleasant experience it is to be so close to someone without a scar-marked or damaged face. Especially a woman. In fact, Nadia, with her free-flowing movements and lithe gestures is a joy to behold. Unfortunately a little less so to listen to.

Today she seems to have an air of busy-ness about her. As usual she begins to talk at him. 'Do you know,' she says, 'that there are specially constructed gardens in Cambridge for the blind, where they can go to experience the smell of millions of different flowers from all over the world?' Mo's look indicates that he was indeed ignorant of this most delightful of floral aids. She continues to expound her theories, walking round the small clinic with an arrogant toss of her head, before stopping thoughtfully every now and then. In no time at all Mo has, once again, become completely fascinated by her joyous mood and keeps asking her questions to prolong and encourage it.

'One client,' she goes on, 'got so addicted to experiencing life through the nose that he would go on sniffing jaunts.' At this Mo burst out laughing. 'Yes,' says Nadia, 'we can even allow ourselves to laugh in aromatherapy. Unlike other therapies there is still room for humour.' This is said in contradiction to the stern and unsmiling look on her face. 'Then after we have laughed we can put our humour by and surrender our sluggish, fume-laden and limited sense of smell to the vast invigorating, stress-destroying, universal essence.'

Her eyes roll towards the ceiling, presumably at the

thought, and the pink tip of her tongue peeps out of her mouth as it slithers over her plump heart-shaped lips, moistening them before making ready to continue.

'Well, I've heard it all,' says Mo, staring at her as if she were undressing.

'Oh, no,' she says, giving an irritated laugh, 'you haven't quite heard it all yet.' And, taking attentive looking for attentive listening, she launches into a further discourse.

'By the way, how is your back these days?' asks Nadia some time later, as she flits round the clinic with a sweet- smelling spray.

'It's getting better,' replies Mo, settling back more comfortably on the mattress. 'But some days it's . . .'

He tries to go on but Nadia's voice breaks into his sentence. 'People find their way to aromatherapy by many different routes.' Displaced air wafts over Mo's face as she comes to a stop near the head of the table. 'For some it is the pure love of scent, for others it is somewhere to go to pass a pleasant hour.' Mo hears her lighting the incense. 'And of course it has its groupies.' She laughs. 'Those who just spend all their leisure hours going from therapist to therapist.' Mo keeps silent. He does not feel like talking from such a relaxed position. 'And then there are the seekers, those subtle souls who go to any lengths in their quest for the ultimate aroma.'

She sniffs slowly and dreamily at such an appetising thought. Then, turning down the lights, moves towards the door, adding as she leaves, 'But last, though not least of course, are those who simply need the service.' The tip of the incense stick glows softly in the dark as she closes the door.

When she returns Mo is in that cosy state between dreaming and waking. A really exquisite smell pierces his mind as Nadia releases from an ampoule a tiny droplet under his nose. 'It's called Nagchampa,' she says as Mo opens his eyes. 'It comes from India. All my clients like Nagchampa. Somehow it's so artificially natural. Yes. How odd of my clients to surround themselves and their homes with natural things, yet lead such unnatural lives. One of my clients suffers from terrible pains in his joints every time he visits his local health-food shop. He agonises how he can ever possibly afford to keep meeting their rising prices. Such a nice man too. He's a writer. So sensitive. He comes twice a week, seeking refuge from his worries and inspiration for his writing in the fragrances. A true seeker.'

There is a noise outside and Hadrian shouts through the door, 'I'm going out for a while.'

'Don't be too long,' she shouts back. Turning to face Mo again she continues, 'Hadrian's got such a nice small nose.'

Yes, thinks Mo ruefully, a nice small nose and a big loud mouth. Brought up to be non-sexist and non-racist to people of his own class – a bastard to everyone else.

Nadia's voice interrupts his thought. 'Now breathe in deeply,' she says, and any stray marauding tension still lingering in his back seems to be completely disappearing with each outward breath. 'That's it,' she says. 'It's really very simple. Now lie back again and relax. The tension's falling away.' Mo complies with her instructions and when the treatment is over indeed feels that this is so.

He feels so stress-free that he decides to prolong his walk to the station by taking the long way round, strolling leisurely in the gathering twilight. He notices for the first time that the streets are wider, the houses larger than in his own area. Deep in thought he soon loses his way, not realising it until a car brakes violently a few yards in front of him.

Mo's stomach muscles tighten as a big bloke sticks his head out of the passenger seat window, beckoning him over with a nod. Most people ask for directions politely. This one does not. Mo doesn't waste time feigning ignorance. He knows who it is.

'Where you going? And what are you doing in this area?' asks the man, with something between a smile and a snarl.

If you're working you're legal, thinks Mo, telling him his business with great relish.

'OK. Let's see what you've got on you,' continues the copper, getting out and at the same time indicating Mo's pockets with a terse nod of the head as if defying him to refuse. Mo pulls the contents of a pocket out with his right hand and spreads them on the bonnet of the car for all the world to see. The plain-clothes man runs his eyes over them. A notebook. A pen. A comb. Some loose change. 'Got any proof of identity on you?' asks the copper impatiently.

'Yes,' says Mo with a surge of confidence, at the same time pulling from his left-hand pocket the tube pass. The copper's eyes bulge at the sight of Mo's photo, head obscured now by a soft lump of Cheddar cheese.

'Here,' says the copper, 'that's not you.'

'Yeah, it is, guv,' says Mo, flustered with embarrassment.

'What happened to your hair, then?' enquires the copper, smirking with mock concern. Mo feels on safer ground now that the ridiculous has entered the picture. The copper's question shows that he's eased up a bit. A joke might be in order.

'I forgot to put the Grecian in this morning. Never thought I'd meet anyone nice today.'

The copper in the car gives a loud guffaw.

'You didn't, eh?' muses his sidekick, studying Mo's face and weighing up his clothes. Mo holds his tongue, hoping they'll be satisfied just to play their old police games.

'So, who's this woman you're . . . uh, working for? What's her name?' asks the cop, warming again to his quizzing.

'Nadia,' says Mo, feeling foolish. 'I don't know her surname.'

'Nadia, eh? That sounds nice. Don't that sound nice, Joe?' he enquires, turning to his mate who is idly picking his teeth with a match. 'And you're doing the garden for her, are you?'

Before Mo can reply, the cop bursts out laughing as his mate shouts loudly from the car, ''Ere, she's not Lady Chatterley, is she?' Mo laughs too, but they are not finished with the questions.

'Is your job an official appointment?' asks the copper in what passes for a serious tone.

'No, of course not,' says Mo. It's obvious they mean to give him the full wind-up.

'Any chance of promotion? Pension scheme? Paid holidays? That sort of thing?' goes on the cop, with a hard frown as if worried that Mo might get duped. Mo shakes his head, a sudden surge of annoyance pumping through him. 'You want to look into things like that,' continues the CID man, nodding gravely to his mate.

'Yes. Check the job description before you start or you could find yourself bound out of hand for a fiver a week to some neurotic woman for life.'

The cop in the car bursts out laughing. Mo has to laugh too at the improbability of the copper's joke. Then, bored with baiting, the copper gets back into the car and, without another word, they drive off.

Mo does not dawdle now. The birds have stopped chirping as he hurries towards the tube – unlike the birds in the treetops on council estates which twitter all night through, confused by the artificial light. When he finally reaches his stop he goes into a shop where he buys a large white loaf, a carton of milk and a huge lump of cheese – the most filling meal he can afford on his limited income – since the mouthwatering smell of unfamiliar spices in Nadia's kitchen has sharpened his appetite.

After a wash and shave Mo makes a pile of sandwiches, half of which he wraps in a brown paper bag for the following day. The remainder he eats for supper. As there are no cooking facilities inside or outside the room, he finishes off his meal with a carton of milk. After the food and drink he doesn't feel so tired and starts to write. Thoughts pour from his mind, racing so fast his pen's left behind. Physical tiredness apart, his target is four pages a day, though sometimes there are as many as six or eight. But by the time he has reworked his initially illegible scrawl, it invariably ends at four. On occasions a sentence presents itself in a variety of ways, none of them wrong, but as Mo gathers confidence, he learns to choose which works best.

In the beginning, lacking more qualified commentators and hoping to gain some useful feedback, Mo would show his former drinking partners his work. They meant well. But, 'Ha, ha, ha, that's a right fucking laugh, Mo. It's fucking good. Have you seen Mad Murphy around lately? The cunt owes me a couple of quid' was not the kind of assessment, however well-intentioned, to encourage his best work.

Aiming at more academic critics Mo began showing his stuff to the drop-out drug addicts who squat on his old haunts. Their assessments being more penetrating (and therefore to Mo's eyes more valid) he was overjoyed until the following day when their judgements changed, owing to their being on a higher or lower plane. Mo has to attend to every word – a hazardous task without a sounding board, trying to generate positive criticisms from within.

Today he arrives at his stop with over half an hour to spare. He waits in the living room and makes himself tea – his regular beverage since giving up the drink. How quickly the reserve has broken down. The invisible barrier that stands between the worker and his boss. That area of unfamiliarity where no quarter is given or asked. And as Mo has become more familiar with her ways, Nadia has started to lose her allure. He no longer feels it as real concern when she asks how he feels. Whatever he answer, he receives the same mechanical smile showing she's not been concentrating on her question, nor paying any attention to his answers. He's also noticed lately that when he is working in the garden her hearing seems to be deteriorating too and he's had to shout or go up close to make himself heard. And since her normally loud voice begins to lose its volume at the most inconvenient times it forces him to leave whatever he is doing and go over to wherever she happens to be. This is causing tension to build up again, making him edgy. Since, in the absence of sound, he's taken to lip reading as best he can, watching her mouth is beginning to cause all kinds of complications as he goes about his work. But it is preferable to being tapped silently on the shoulder and, turning, find her standing there, frowning with annoyance or shaking her head in feigned tolerance over some trivial offence. It is no joke, looking for a bit of peace and quiet while trying to work only to be rounded on with a lot of petulant heat.

He isn't proof, however, against her sophisticated bearing, or her coaxing little words, and whenever he veers towards mentioning her subjugational attitudes, she woos him back with pleasantries and jokes. It is beginning to look very much as though the only give and take there is ever going to be in the relationship is that she gives offence easily and takes it easier still. Under these circumstances Mo has decided he will finish the job he's started but does not intend to continue as gardener.

His mind stuffed with promises and unfulfilled hopes Mo journeys back and forth on the tube to Nadia's house each day. During this time a girl, her skirt caught in the suck of the wind that follows the train, is dragged to her death. Another's dress is torn off in a three-minute rape between stations.

Mo is greeted as he gets to the door one day by Hadrian and Nadia, both bubbling with excitement. 'Hello, Mo. Meet our new addition to the family. Now we shan't be bored!'

Mo looks to where she's pointing at a large brown puppy lapping noisily at a bowl of water. Seeing Mo, the dog makes straight for him. Tail wagging, frantic with friendliness, jumping up and placing its two enormous paws on Mo's shoulders, slobbering great dollops of saliva down the front of his clothes, saturating his coat sleeves and hands. Mo keeps patting the dog, holding his own head back, twisting it this way and that, trying to avoid the canine kiss. He's becoming very tense. Surely the boy can see that he's not enjoying the dog's insistence on heavy petting? Yet neither Hadrian nor Nadia make any move to his aid. Instead, both are doubled up laughing and shaking with delight at the dog's antics and Mo's flustered attempts to avoid them. To make matters worse, Mo is trying to do too many things at once. Stay calm, be polite and get out of the dog's clutches – and not necessarily in that order. If this dog had been in the street Mo would have stepped back and lashed out with his foot.

Eventually Mo manages, with great difficulty and repeated effort, to push the dog away.

'Oh, you've tired poor Floppy out, Mo,' says Nadia, making clicking noises with her mouth and looking with concern at her new family member.

'He don't half like getting his own way,' says Mo, breathlessly.

Choosing to ignore this, Nadia begins opening a huge tin of dog food, throwing a question over her shoulder at Hadrian. 'How far did you walk him today?' Hadrian, who is fiddling with the telly controls, pays her no heed. She finally addresses herself to Mo. 'The new lawn mower is in the shed. If—'

Mo is up before she can finish the sentence. 'Right. I'll get on with it,' he says, moving towards the french windows. He has been looking forward to using the new machine ever since the old petrol one packed up some time ago.

Mo pulls the gleaming mower from the shed, runs the lead back through the window, plugs in, switches on, and begins. But it turns out to be one of those electric machines that hardly cut. The shield is missing too, which allows the blades to spray showers of mown grass in all directions. You can't beat nature, though! thinks Mo happily. The smell is so nice – until a shower of minced grass and moist dog shit hits him smack in the mouth, the stench half suffocating him as it slithers down his chin.

'What a shame,' says Nadia when he tells her about it. 'The trouble is, you see, your nose is still acting as a sensual inhibitor.' Mo looks at her open-mouthed.

'It hasn't quite entered your consciousness yet that all smells are ultimately the same. Your enthusiasm is marred only by your inexperience. Everything will work out fine if you just hunt down that missing shield.' She gestures vaguely in the direction of the shed. 'Fix it on the mower and the machine will do the rest.'

'But the dog's stuff is all over the ground and when I—'

'What are you talking about?' she snaps, jumping in before he can finish. 'Hadrian's cleared it all away. It's part of his Saturday job.' Mo is about to complain that although Hadrian might be the last word in Saturday jobs, the dog shit still remains. But Nadia's ominous silence, hands on hips, glowering, tells him all he needs to know and he realises that he has just been landed with another unpaid job. Seeing that he remains standing there with something of a perplexed look on his face, Nadia softens, telling him to make himself a cup of tea before he starts work again. 'And there's some nice pâté in the fridge, too. Make yourself a snack,' she coaxes.

After brewing the tea Mo sits down at the table mumbling something to himself. It isn't grace before meals.

Just as he is about to bite into a wedge of pâté and bread, Nadia, who had left the room, comes rushing back looking flustered. 'Oh, Mo, I'm terribly sorry,' she says, moving up close to where he is sitting, 'but before you start eating could you just give me a hand to carry Floppy out to the garden?' Clearly out of his element, Mo's silent mumblings become more animated as he starts to rise. He pushes away from the table, absent-mindedly putting the sandwich he was about to devour clumsily into his jacket pocket. Nadia, clearly surprised by this unexpected show of agitation, moves still nearer, viewing every mannerism attentively. Assured within the protective cocoon of her own authority against any form of rebellion, especially verbal, she continues to observe him. Had he deliberately set out to amuse her he couldn't have done it better. Fumbling, frowning, lips moving soundlessly, face flushed, eyes flashing with impotent rage and embarrassment. And for no visible reason, she thinks, smiling tolerantly, as if such ramblings, though not to be indulged, are yet understandable in working-class males. 'He's so lazy,' she says, humouring Mo, 'that it's becoming quite a feat to get him to walk from the living room to the garden just to do his business every day.'

'What a nuisance,' replies Mo, thawing a bit towards her.

'I couldn't possibly budge him on my own,' she adds as they come up to Floppy. 'But with a big strong man like you it should be no trouble.'

Mo, flattered, bends down towards the dog, placing his hands on each side of its large hindquarters and begins to push him towards the street door which Nadia holds open. The dog, flattening its rump, allows itself to be pushed along the floor – in fact it seems to enjoy it, becoming so relaxed that his head starts to wobble, bobbing up and down like a toy in the back of a car window.

To pass the time as he waits for his treatment, Mo wanders upstairs, tea in hand, to search the empty rooms for some misplaced garden tools Nadia asked him to find. So many people homeless, thinks Mo, and these rooms lying empty. He swallows mouthfuls of tea to clear his throat of the billowing dust clouds which keep churning up as he searches for the tools. Locating first a damaged billhook he glances down into the half-finished garden. Should he finish the mug of tea, or should he leave half? Mo, preoccupied with the thought, does not hear Nadia call out to him. What if he wants the toilet half-way through the treatment? Perhaps better not to finish the tea? As he muses, Nadia's voice, much stronger now, reaches his ears.

'Coming,' he shouts, making for the clinic, standing smartly to one side of the hallway to allow Nadia's last client to pass: a tall well-dressed man who gives him an indifferent look as he leaves. Some of the clients show by an occasional, stiff-faced, reluctant nod that they recognise Mo as the gardener. But only seldom do any of them speak. Perhaps they are annoyed that Nadia leaves them alone in the clinic far more often these days, apparently on Mo's account, while she wanders out to view or supervise the rapid changes he is making in the garden. If Mo makes any attempt to speak to them they withdraw so haughtily that he soon learns to make himself scarce when anyone is about.

'Goodness me,' she exclaims as Mo comes through the door. 'Your clothes are all covered in dog hairs.'

'I never noticed,' says Mo, flustered now by the shocked look on her face.

'You mustn't bring them in here,' she continues, flicking her hands disdainfully at him. 'Brush yourself off in the garden.'

Mo spins round with embarrassment, making for the garden as if he's been caught urinating up against an operating theatre wall while delicate surgery is in progress. When he returns, after satisfying herself of his hairlessness, she beckons him to be seated.

'Sorry about that,' says Mo as he sits down.

'Oh, not to worry,' replies Nadia, pouring some liquid from a large bottle into a smaller one. 'Cleanliness is quite a problem, particularly in the summer when it's warm. One can't really leave the door open for fear of clients getting hay fever and the breeze blowing twigs and petals in. I'm afraid it makes me very cross. Still, what would we do without gardens?' She smiles, without regard to the fact that most people have no garden. 'What an eyesore, and how depressing it must be to live in those council blocks. So vulgar-looking, and why, for heaven's sake, couldn't they have put more thought into working out their aspects?'

Mo keeps looking at her, intrigued, even though he isn't quite sure what she's on about. She smiles grimly. 'They block out what little sunlight we get, leaving large areas round about them devoid of any foliage or grass. So much concrete. Oh, that reminds me . . .' she says suddenly, stopping her pacing and pulling a mauve envelope from a pocket hidden in the folds of her dress. 'Will you post this on your way home for me?' she asks, handing the envelope to Mo. 'It's my monthly donation to Window Box Link Up.' Mo smiles at her but makes no comment as she goes on, 'The trust was set up to encourage householders and local councils to plant more grass, trees and shrubbery everywhere.'

'I hope no acorns fall into the window boxes,' returns Mo mischievously. But, noting her tightened jaw, adds quietly, 'It sounds like a very nice idea.'

'Yes,' she says. 'I've adopted the trust as my ideal.'

The sergeant looks all in as he swings in off the central concourse with the new constable.

'Lots of strange faces out there tonight, sarge,' remarks the duty officer.

'Yeah. More nouveau roughs. Station's getting flooded with 'em. Pass me the Scrabble board,' he growls, tired out after coming in off his rounds. 'We'll play in the Interrogation Room, constable. It's quieter in there,' he remarks to his latest prodigy as he unlocks the door. Inside, the room is bare except for a wooden table and two chairs. A metal filing cabinet completes the furnishings. 'Pass me that rule book,' says the sergeant, lowering himself into a chair. 'Never go far wrong in this life if you stick to the rules,' he adds, patting the book fondly as they begin to play. But it is far from easy since the sergeant has difficulty in spelling and the constable with counting, and extraordinary complications begin to arise during the game. They are just trying to sort out one of their more minor mistakes, like whose turn it is to play, when a loud bang outside makes them jump. The phone begins ringing insistently. As the sergeant picks it up he nods, indicating with his head for the constable to hide the Scrabble board.

'Yes, sir, a bomb . . . yes, sir . . . you want a body . . . anything else, sir? . . . OK, got it, yes, sir, we'll soon have it cleared up.' Putting the phone down, he turns to the recruit. 'Right, constable, there's been a bomb scare. Get moving, get a body.'

They make for the door. The constable stops suddenly: a thought has occurred to him. 'Who, sarge?'

'Anybody . . . Oh, make sure he's got an Irish accent.'

They leave.

After a while they come back with a nattily dressed black bloke wearing a baker-boy cap. They sit him on a chair, both

105

watching him. The constable gets a notebook out. Waiting, biro poised.

'Name?'

The man's head jerks up, dreadlocks swirling. 'Leroy Webb.'

'Don't give us that shit, Paddy. I'm not in the mood,' says the sergeant.

Leroy is shocked. 'My name's not Paddy. I ain't even got an Irish accent.'

'That can be arranged.'

'What you talking about, man?' shrieks Leroy in helpless bewilderment.

'Elocution lessons.'

The constable is impressed. 'Brilliant, sarge, and deportment training. One shoulder higher than the other, throw in a nice wardrobe, pair of hobnails and a donkey jacket. He'll be ready for his coming out party – Number One Court Wednesday morning.'

The sergeant puts up a restraining hand, smiling patiently at this show of youthful enthusiasm. 'Not so fast, not so fast. Let's not get carried away. Heat of the moment. Emotional shock. Do something rash. Regrettable, even. But I do sympathise with your feelings. I've met this type before. Starts by throwing a squib or two every bonfire night . . .'

Leroy stirs. 'What you mean? You can't get away with this. You think I'm green?'

'Get that last word down, constable – it's significant.'

The constable scribbles.

'You Protestant or Catholic?'

Leroy gives a sideways look of distaste. 'I ain't neither.'

The sergeant scratches his temple. 'Well, can't really say I blame you. I've never been overfond of rituals myself. All them funny handshakes on Lodge nights. Still, we got to put something down. Can't go before a fine old judge like a complete heathen . . . puts them off, see? All that money wasted on missionaries in the past. What was your father?'

'My father was an elder in the First Pentecostal Non-Sectarian Baptist Church.'

'Well, I've heard everything now,' says the sergeant, looking over at Leroy as if he's just become a marvel to him.

Leroy is getting impatient. 'May I ask why I have been forced to come here?'

'Let's not say forced,' pleads the sergeant mockingly, 'let's just say you have been invited.'

Leroy is surprised. 'Invited! You mean like for tea perhaps.'

'Oh, you'll certainly be staying for tea.'

'What am I accused of?'

'Nothing . . . yet.'

'Then why are you holding me?'

'We're holding you under Article 12.'

'I ain't done anything.'

They wait. A long pause – an old copper's trick. The sergeant raises his eyebrows. 'You mean to tell me that you have never committed a crime in your life?'

'No, never.'

The sergeant shakes his head in disbelief. 'I don't understand this . . . Are you trying to tell me that you've never broke the law ever? Even when you was a kid?'

'Well, perhaps silly things as a child,' answers Leroy.

The sergeant is obviously relieved. 'Phew. I thought my faith in human nature was about to be destroyed.'

'How long you going to keep me here?' asks Leroy. 'It's against the law,' he adds, hoping to appeal to reason.

The sergeant and constable look aghast. 'What law?' says the sergeant, lighting a cigarette and giving one to the constable. 'We can hold you *sine die*.'

'What?'

'Indefinitely, old son. Try you when you're ninety. Give you eight lifers. Unless, of course . . .' He places a sheet of paper in front of the suspect. 'Look, what's needed here, and would be ideal,' says the sergeant, flipping on the reading lamp and aiming it right into Leroy's face, 'is a little statement . . . just a few words. Nothing too creative.'

Leroy looks at him stunned.

'Tell you what. I'll put a few words down myself. Help your inspiration. OK?'

'No, man.'

'Come, come. What you got – writer's block? Try, don't be bashful. We all know what sensitive souls writers can be. Oh, yes, the times I've sat up all night with them, giving them mental and physical encouragement, fetching them cups of tea, lights for their fags.'

Leroy pulls out a packet. 'Can I have a light then, please?'

The sergeant makes as if to offer one but is interrupted by the excited constable. 'Excuse me, sarge, that will not be possible in this case as, in conjunction with Article 12, Rule 4 applies, along with Clauses 12, 18, 20, 26 and on through to Subsection 82.'

'Bless me, constable. What you on about? I've always looked after the welfare of my prisoners, yes indeed. Their absolute comfort has always been ever dearest to my heart.'

The constable smiles carefully. 'Of course, sarge, your kindness is legendary.' The sergeant looks smug as the constable continues. 'But in this particular case, the offering of naked lights could be considered *prima facie* evidence of conspiracy with or without premeditatory collusion as intent to provide accused with the means to manufacture an incendiary device.'

The sergeant is clearly bewildered. 'Oh, dear me, you are getting ahead of me, constable.' He shakes his head. 'I must be getting old. The young police mind . . . so clear, untarnished, spotless. Pure, even.' He trains his eyes on Leroy, slowly blowing a stream of smoke into his face. 'He won't allow me to deviate or bend the rules one iota.'

Leroy's expression becomes pained as the cigarette smoke lingers in the air. He stares at the sergeant longingly.

'I know they're bad,' says the sarge. 'I should quit . . .'

'Please. Can I have a smoke? Just one little light won't harm,' pleads Leroy.

'No, we got to go by the rules. We're fair men . . . British bobbies. Fairest in the world. Just remember that. Don't even carry guns . . . well, not where you can see them anyway.'

The constable started to make himself busy again. 'Where are the charge sheets, sarge?'

'In the cabinet, as I remember well. I never forget, Hendon-trained originally, stands to a good copper. You know.'

'Whereabouts . . . in there, sarge?'

'In the top half . . .' He puts his hand to his head. 'Or was it in the bottom?'

The constable comes back, putting a blank charge sheet on the table as the sergeant asks him irritably, 'Where's that tea lady tonight?'

'She's off sick, sarge.'

'Sick? She's always off sick. What's wrong with her this time?'

The constable shuffles his feet with embarrassment. 'I don't know,' he stammers.

'I think it's premeditated!' explodes the sergeant. 'Always happens on her bingo night,' he adds peevishly, looking suspiciously at the suspect.

'Yeah. I know what you're thinking, 'cause I used to think the same thing myself once.'

Leroy is scared, not wanting to fall out with him.

'You don't remember me, do you, lad?' smiles the sergeant slyly.

'Well, I'm not sure . . .' answers Leroy, hesitantly.

The sergeant smiles again. 'Course you're not, 'cause we never met before.'

Leroy looks confused. 'Never mind,' adds the sergeant, continuing in a more friendly tone. 'What do you work at, lad?'

'I'm a motor mechanic.'

'Excellent. A good trade that. Stands to a man. Good wages too . . . I should imagine,' he probes.

'Not bad,' replies Leroy, feeling on safer ground here.

'Good.' The sergeant nods his head at him, then pauses to think before going on. 'I don't pretend to be an intellectual,' he says with a superior air, 'but wasn't it Einstein who said that electricity was an absolute? Well, he should have included money as well 'cause that's also an absolute. An absolute necessity.' He looks at Leroy. 'Stop me if I'm going too fast, but how shall I put it . . .? It's a little-known fact that in certain delicate circumstances money has been known to pass hands, thereby granting person or persons, known or unknown, immunity from prosecution. There, I've said it! Of course, this case is a little awkward, being as how it's political and all that. But then so's kicking the cat if it happens to belong to the Pakistani High Commissioner . . . To put it bluntly, some ask for immunity from prosecution at this juncture. Can do . . . but it costs.'

'I haven't got anything and I'm innocent.' Leroy looks trapped.

'You're beginning to sound very unsuitable.'

'He's beginning to look unsuitable, too, sarge.'

'He certainly lacks something . . .' says the sergeant, shaking his head in feigned despair. 'Never mind, I'm sure it'll come to me. You know, it's a funny thing, constable . . .'

'Yes, sarge?' The two coppers' glances cross.

'Yes, indeed. Not funny ha ha – not that sort of funny – but we're all sitting here and I don't know if I'm a bit psychic or what, but I get a distinctly uncomfortable feeling that one of us is emitting hostile vibrations. Weird really, when you come to think of it, 'cause there ain't any need for enmity here.'

'No, course not, sarge.'

'No, definitely not. 'Tain't like we was all from separate planets or something . . .'

In the pause that follows the constable answers with undoubted enthusiasm, 'My mother was Irish.'

'Hear that. Why, I do believe I've got some Irish blood in me old veins too. Come to think of it, yes indeed, wasn't my great-great-grandfather on my mother's side from Dublin? Well, well, well. Don't that take the biscuit? Why, we're just one big happy family after all. A right load of old blarney he used to talk . . . always on about the Cause he was. Same as you, lads, only it's a new cause, nowadays,

I suppose.' He bends down enquiringly over the suspect. 'Eh, son?'

'I don't know what you on about. Closest I've ever been to any cause was over the Elephant and Castle way.'

The sergeant is immediately interested. 'Oh, yes, lad, and which Cause would that be?'

'Newington Causeway.'

The sergeant walks over to the filing cabinet. 'Keep an eye on the prisoner, constable. They sometimes injure themselves trying to stand up too fast,' he says. Taking out a truncheon from the cabinet drawer he saunters back to the table. 'Only a few times I've had to put it about,' he says, patting the truncheon in the palm of his hand. 'Primitive system, really. Too many side-effects. All right for them Argentinian juntas, but a bit too crude for over here, I'm afraid . . . breaks resistance though . . . but in the process distorts the memory banks. Sometimes damaging the brain . . . nuisance, really, as the information often comes out too garbled . . . gibberish mumblings, hardly acceptable in an English court of law. Still, a lot of the lads in the Met swear by it. But I like to keep in fashion, move with the times.' He looks at the truncheon. 'Yes, me old beauty, you've been superseded by the old punishment and reward game. Hot and cold, on and off. But in an emergency you can still produce results.'

Leroy is now very scared. 'Listen, man. I'd tell you government secrets if I knew any. But I don't. I don't know anything. I'm innocent.'

The sergeant shakes his head wearily. 'The plain fact is that judges like guilty pleas, and some people need help in making up their own mind.' He places the truncheon on the table where Leroy can't do a thing but stare at it. 'We want you to unwind.'

'Oh, no, I don't need any help with my mind. I know I'm innocent.'

'A real positive thinker, eh? Hear that, constable?'

'Yes, sarge.'

'Yes, indeed, we could do with a man like that in the Force.'

111

'Oh no, in future I ain't going to be seen out after dark. I'm innocent.'

The sergeant's face screws up at this as if he's just been sucking a lemon. 'If you keep coming out with statements like that you won't have a future. You won't even have a past.'

Just then the phone begins to ring. The sergeant bends to answer it. 'Hello. Yes, of course I remember him, it was only last night . . . he's in where? What, council care? Oh, intensive care? Well he should be a bit more co-operative when he comes out of there. All right, yeah. Got another stroppy one tonight. Why's it always me that gets all the hard cases?' He slams the phone down.

'Trouble, sarge?'

'I wouldn't say that, no. On your night off I had a wino in here for a "drunk and incapable" . . . stupid bastard really. Ended up on the life-support machine. Attacked ten of my officers, he did . . . dented Constable Klint's boots so badly we had to issue him an emergency chit for a new pair. Caused a hell of a stink with the clothing store manager I can tell you, 'cause the soles and heels were in perfect condition, see?'

Leroy pulls himself up in the chair, becoming proudly aggressive. 'I'm not having this. I'm innocent. You don't worry me.'

'Strength of character is to be admired.' The sergeant speaks resignedly. 'And in times of war would probably earn you a medal.' He waits before continuing viciously, 'But at this particular moment in time, old son, I'm afraid it'll only earn you a fucking good kicking.' He suddenly lashes out with his foot, kicking something under the table. It makes a frightening noise and Leroy jumps. 'I can never understand why criminals who haven't got the energy to go down the road for a loaf of bread for their mothers will fight tooth and nail against any form of committal proceedings that can only be, in the long run, to their advantage,' ends the sergeant, flicking a fag at the constable and sticking another into his own mouth.

'Perhaps some . . .' says the constable hesitantly, picking up the fag and at the same time offering the sergeant a light.

'Well, one or two . . . may not feel quite guilty enough to see it that way, sarge?'

The constable, his recent college training coming to the fore, is about to go on but the sergeant, obviously in the habit of having his remarks confirmed, begins speaking quietly. 'Not having had the somewhat dubious benefit of an academic upbringing, constable, I'll not pretend to understand that last statement. So say it again, but this time say it in plain, truthful, proper Queen's English. Right?'

'Ah, yes, sarge . . . obviously,' the constable hems and haws, 'obviously I've mistaken what you said. A bit Mutt and Jeff in the right ear. Damp weather activates the wax.'

The sergeant smiles indulgently. 'Try wearing a scarf. You gotta keep well wrapped up this weather.'

'Yes, sarge. Thank you, sarge.'

'It's quite all right, lad. Feel free. Feel free. I like a questioning mind, but anyone who's brought in here's a criminal.'

'How d'you reach that conclusion?' demands Leroy, forgetting his fear in a wave of anger that rises up inside him suddenly.

'Simple. He establishes his own guilt by coming through that door. Being coy, playing hard to get, and generally giving everybody a bad time.'

In the heavy silence that follows all three look at one another with fascination.

'I haven't done anything,' says Leroy flatly.

The sergeant, now barely able to control his fury, replies, 'Thinking of yourself as innocent's like saying I don't want to go out to play today, I'm a spoilsport. It's a negative state of mind. Twisted . . . yes, that's what it is. Limp, whingeing and twisted. A proper man – that is, a real man with a strong character – takes charge of his own destiny, he doesn't have to be helped. No, he draws himself up. He realises at last, "If the police have brought me here they must have had a very good reason, so I'm not going to be a shit, an 'orrible ineffectual little shit, whose only ambition in life is to try and fuck some poor old overworked police sergeant about. No." A strong person says to himself, "I'm

113

too honourable for that kind of hypocrisy. I'm bigger than that, I'm positive, I'm truthful." ' The sergeant is frothing at the mouth, lost in his madness. ' "I'm guilty! Guilty! Say it, son, it'll help you. Oh, it'll give you such relief. It'll be like a spiritual awakening. Oh, the times I've seen it happen. Up all night with the accused, who've been proclaiming their innocence ... Ah, how I hate the sound of that word, it's like a blasphemy ... leaves such a bad taste in the mouth ...' He pauses. 'Where was I? Oh, yes, about four in the morning, they starts thrashing about like madmen, wrestling with their own stupidity and stubbornness ... Suddenly, their eyes become glazed. They stare about, not aware of themselves or their surroundings, oblivious to all. At this point I've had to catch a lot of them in a half-nelson ... stop them injuring themselves. Just as I've got my knee in their kidneys, awareness dawns. Slowly at first, oh, ever so slowly, helped by my fatherly and protective grasp, they begin to see the light ... the reason why ... what it's all about. "Guilty," they screams, "Guilty." I have a hell of a job to stop them then ...'

The sergeant pauses, shaking his head, thinking. The other two stare at him silently. Eventually the constable breaks the silence. 'Beautiful, sarge. Why it's bordering on metaphysics!' he says in a voice trembling with awe.

'I try my best. That's all I can do. But it don't seem to be good enough.' He looks around slowly as if saddened by what he sees. The constable replies gently, 'I'm sure your efforts are appreciated, sarge.'

'I don't know. They seem to mistrust my motives.'

'It's because they've mixed with the rougher elements all their lives, sarge. Never met anyone they could confide in. No one as sensitive as you, that is. Comes as a bit of a shock to them, I suppose.'

This perks up the sergeant.

'Yes, that must be it. Never met anyone they could trust. Why, if I wasn't a fair copper there's a whole list of delaying tactics I could subject them to.'

'What are they, sarge?' asks the constable, with the manic zeal displayed only by the most attentive of students.

'Well,' replies the sergeant, lighting up another smoke, 'you can leave the court just before their case is brought up, with a message that you've been called out on another case at another court. This merits an automatic custodial remand. Next time the accused appears you suddenly take sick leave, occasioning a further mandatory remand. On subsequent appearances, you tell the old beak that you're making further inquiries in the case, implying that these will result in further charges being brought, always with the proviso, of course, that you're pending this and pending that. By the way, this is a good one 'cause it allows you to get acquainted with the missus and kids again and do the odd spot of decorating. But suddenly . . . sometimes . . . there's no case to answer on account of you're unable to produce a body at court owing to death by misadventure. I've made a few contributions to this clause in the past. Who hasn't? Three suicides, two Acts of God, and four fell down the stairs. You wouldn't credit the lack of balance among the criminal fraternity. Still, that's all behind me now. I was young then . . . had a high sense of duty.'

'What are we to conclude from all that, sarge?' asks the constable quietly, as if he's just been handed the secret of the universe but isn't quite sure if he wants it.

'Conclude?' The sergeant frowns. 'Why, nothing, constable . . . nothing at all.'

Interrogation rooms are not built to keep suspects comfortable. Leroy is beginning to wilt. 'I want to speak to a lawyer,' he says suddenly.

They look at him in amazement, as if seeing him for the first time.

'Hear that, constable?'

'Yes, sarge.'

'He wants to speak to a lawyer. Notice anything odd about that statement?'

The constable hesitates. He's not on firm ground here. 'I . . . ah . . . I'm not sure.'

'Well, I'll tell you. Notice he doesn't want to speak to his mother, or his father, his wife, or even his lover.'

'Perhaps he's got a boyfriend, sarge?' the constable laughs.

'Yes, but he doesn't want to speak to him. No. Who's the only person he wants to speak to? A lawyer. Now, it's been my not inconsiderable experience that only people troubled by guilty conscience speak to lawyers 'cause innocent people don't need 'em. They're far too expensive. What innocent person's going to throw away all his hard-earned money on something he don't need in the first place?'

'Your methods of deduction are amazing, sarge. We never learned anything like that at training college.'

The sergeant gives him a comradely look. 'Years of experience, lad,' he says. 'Course I'm not against the judiciary, oh, no, they've got their jobs to do. We've got ours. And it's a very heart-warming sight after days spent interrogating a suspect to see his lawyer come swaggering through them doors, throwing writs of Habeas Corpus about like they were confetti – only to be informed that, in his absence, his client has changed his plea and signed a full confession.'

The silence runs on until Leroy blurts out anxiously. 'I know my rights. I want a lawyer now.'

The sergeant looks at him menacingly. 'You've been out in the sun?'

'I already told you I come from Jamaica.'

'There's a lot of sun there. You've caught a tan all right. Package tour?'

'I was born there.'

'If you persist with this attitude I'm going to have to charge you with trying to confuse the police and pervert the course of justice. I'm in no mood to take any more of your nonsense tonight, lad. I want some plain answers. Otherwise . . . I'm afraid I'll get very cross. Now, constable, where did you leave them unsigned confessions?'

'It escapes me for the moment, sarge.'

The sergeant looks significantly at the suspect before he speaks. 'Well, you better not let anything else escape you tonight, lad.'

As they sit looking at each other the phone rings. The

116

sergeant answers it. 'Hello. Yes, Bill . . . No, no trouble.' He looks at the suspect. 'Well, it's a bit drastic that. No, I think we can manage for the moment, anyway. Yes? Oh, you did . . . ? Splendid, splendid. OK, Bill. Night.' Turning to the constable he speaks. 'My old mate, Bill, the gaoler, he's just bought his fourth house. By the way, you married, constable?'

'Not yet, sarge. Can't afford it. We're saving for a house.'

The sergeant gives him a fatherly look. 'Once you get to know the ropes you'll have no financial worries in this job. I bought my own semi, a car and a nice little caravan at Southend during my all too brief period as custodian of prisoners' property. Spot of bother with the treasurer. Still, prices were lower then. Everything's gone up these days. Everything, that is, except the criminal mentality.' Leroy takes a coughing fit, putting his hand to his mouth to suppress it. 'What's up? Something gone down the wrong way?' asks the sergeant menacingly.

Leroy nods vigorously, then they sit silently. Suddenly three loud bangs ring out causing the sergeant and constable to jump. 'Oh, no. Not another one . . .' moans the sergeant as the telephone almost lifts them out of their seats.

'Yes . . . oh, good evening, inspector. What?' His head jerks back and he stares at the mouthpiece. 'But I've . . .' He is clearly flustered. 'Well, of course. That is a relief, sir. What about the suspect, sir? All a mistake. Just a car backfiring. Well, that *is* good news . . . aah, not good news, sir. Your car . . . Just a second, sir.' He cunningly thinks to himself. 'I may be able to help you there, sir. Leave it to me. Good night, sir.'

He slams the phone down and looks straight at Leroy. 'Well, Mr Webb, it seems there's been a small mistake. Sorry to have detained you, but . . . you know, trial and error.'

He can't be transferred to paperwork, thinks the constable, because he can't bloody read . . .

'May I go now?' asks Leroy, rising disgustedly.

'Yes, of course.'

As Leroy walks to the door the sergeant follows , putting

his arm around the other man's shoulder. 'There's just one thing more before you go . . .' Leroy looks at him suspiciously. 'Mechanic, you said you were?'

'Yes,' answers Leroy in an uncertain voice.

'Good, good . . . Constable?'

'Yes, sarge.'

'Take Mr Webb down to the garage to meet Inspector Perkins.'

'Yes, sarge.'

The constable eventually returns to find the sergeant pacing the floor in agitated confusion, as if he's just been at a failed picnic.

'Everything OK down there?' he snaps.

'Yes,' replies the constable, giving the sergeant a meaningful look. 'He's fixing the exhaust for the inspector now!' He's never realised the Force was so incestuous, passing suspects around among brother officers to use and abuse. Still, waste not, want not . . .

'Good. Well, we've wasted a lot of time here and we still got that brothel case them Eyeties was running from that ice-cream van. A dead giveaway that – every time the music started up all the fathers would run out of their council flats for a lick of a strawberry split.'

'Wasn't there a witness for the police coming forward, sarge?'

'Yes, constable. Italian Laura. But she's done a bunk. We need another body for Court Two in the morning.' He shakes his head wearily. 'Phew, give me a straightforward case of mass murder any time.'

'What happens if you can't get a body, sarge?'

The sergeant's eyes narrow. 'That's never happened before.'

'Well, it seems to have happened now,' smirks the constable.

The sergeant smiles grimly, stepping over to the filing cabinet to replace the truncheon. 'Oh, I don't know,' he says, rummaging around absently. Then turning slowly he begins advancing on the constable, a woman's dress in one hand, a pair of high-heeled shoes in the other.

Lucretia is feeling mean this evening. Her Italian blood is well up when she gets into the car to drive over to Nadia's with Max, a writer on one of those fringe magazines. He feels her Continental vibes unsettling him as he makes to help her with the seatbelt – she's in no mood for his wimpish ministrations and fixes him with her 'are we being silly?' stare. Looking directly at her, Max takes in the short, tough hair, swept up and over, the long thin nose, the pursed bloodless lips, and a rather spiteful flash in the eyes.

Max knows better than to try to hold the Loosh's stare too long and, dropping his eyes submissively, kicks at an imaginary object on the floor. He is jarred back to stark reality, however, by her piercing shrieks as she flings open the door and swings two thin but shapely legs on to the road. The cause of her excitement is a black prostitute who has inadvertently placed her hand on the car's bonnet. To steady herself in her tipsy condition, she peers through the windscreen between the numerous anti-racism stickers at Max and Lucretia, whom she has mistaken for a couple of potential clients.

Springing out of the car, the Loosh rushes at her, screeching, with fists clenched. The prostitute is surprised but hardly frightened – in these streets anything is likely to happen. She doesn't attack but, backed up against a wall by the ferocity of this sudden onslaught, lashes out with her fist, catching the Loosh full in the eye. The Loosh flinches but manages to get in a good kick at the pro's shin. Then they both back off, strutting, shaking their heads – for all the world like two fighting cocks. Max moves in to stop them, hoping against hope that they both drop down with fowl pest.

*

119

Mo has been working in the garden for nearly five hours without a break. A small space of time in the course of a year but a long enough span in a day spent fighting his way through the last of the tangled hedge growth with a broken-handled billhook. Now, as the sounds of the party come wafting across the heaps of rubble that he has cleared, he decides to call it quits. As he changes his shoes, Nadia asks him to stay on for a while, her tone a little insistent.

'We're having a party,' she says, drawing him into a dimly lit room. 'And you shall meet Lucretia.' Mo glances at her.

'I think you'll like her. She's got some work for you. Now, something to drink, Mo?'

'No, thanks.'

'Something to eat, then?' She starts piling salad on to a plate without waiting for his reply. 'Have you nearly finished?' she asks, handing him the food with an unhurried movement.

'Yes. Another day should do it.'

She seems not to hear, looking round instead. She shakes her head with a show of weariness as if to clear it. 'Goodness. How I hate parties. People. People . . .'

And Mo's thoughts are about the same as Nadia wanders off to mingle with the other guests. He isn't sure about getting more work but he decides to stay anyway. Who knows? Lucretia might be nice. Better than going back to an empty room.

'Mo, this is Sophie,' says Nadia, as she comes wandering back with a pretty woman of about twenty by her side. Sophie walks with the fluid movements of an alert young panther.

'Hello,' says Mo, reaching out his hand to her, his face flushed with enthusiasm as she sits down.

'Sophie's one of my students,' says Nadia, turning away immediately, her attention distracted elsewhere.

Sophie plucks a little crumb from the corner of her lips as she surveys Mo. 'So you're the gardener?'

'Yes,' says Mo. 'And you're an aromatherapist?'

'Well . . . not quite,' says Sophie, stretching out a hand

and deftly picking from Mo's plate a sliver of cucumber. 'Actually,' she says, popping the cucumber into her mouth and inclining her head so that she can see over Mo's shoulder, 'I really want to be a translator but at present I've only got two languages. Well, two and a half really if you count my African Studies.' And she gives a modest little laugh. Mo gazes intently at her, impressed, as she continues, 'But that's neither here nor there, because I'm going to America in a year's time.'

'Why are you going there?' asks Mo, interest further aroused.

'I'm going into film directing,' says Sophie, waving across the room to someone. 'My father's in it and we are going to make low-budget films about police harassment of the intellectuals in Limpopo.'

'What about all the poorly educated people there? Aren't you going to help them?' asks Mo, pulling a wry face. Someone laughs out loud at the other end of the room.

Sophie shakes her head. 'I couldn't do that. They put me right off.'

'Who?' asks Mo in some surprise. 'The people who need help?'

'No. The people who do the so-called helping. They're all so bourgeois and into money.' She sighs. 'Yes. I'm going over for a long holiday next year and then I'm going to start working with my father.' She turns and looks directly at Mo. 'Ever thought of going to America? It's such a go-ahead country,' she coaxes, as if such a possibility is open to everyone.

'Me?' He laughs. 'I'd have to sleep rough in the Bowery or somewhere.'

'Oh, you poor man,' she teases, taking a radish from his plate. With that she stands up and, munching noisily, pads off.

A tall thin man, hair and clothing disarranged, comes into the room. Mo notes, even from that distance, that Nadia greets him respectfully. Looking around until her glance falls on Mo she comes bearing down on him. 'Mo, this is Anton. Anton, this is Mo.'

Anton gives Mo a pointed stare before mumbling his hello. This done, he begins looking round with a pre-occupied scowl. Mo, through mouthfuls of salad, gathers that Anton is another therapist. Anton turns from Mo to look at the newly arriving guests with the air of a man used to making quick criticisms while avoiding them himself. A woman of about thirty-eight, drink in hand, glides in. Cinderella minus slippers, thinks Mo, looking at her knee-length boots.

'Darling, you look wonderful,' she gushes at Nadia.

'And you look simply ravishing yourself tonight, Anna-belle,' says Nadia sweetly. Mo is introduced to Annabelle.

'This is Mo, he's helping me with the garden.' Mo responds by smiling like a hungry if friendly wolf. Annabelle nods vaguely, without allowing Mo to catch her eye, while continuing to talk to Nadia.

'And how was your trip to the Canaries?'

'Oh, it was wonderful,' replies Annabelle. 'But . . .' Here her voice trails off.

'But what?' asks Nadia with concern, taking Annabelle's hand in both of hers.

'Well, as far as the sun and the sea, the hotel and the food went, it was a dream. So healthy. But the men, ah! God! All those sugar daddies around – you were in constant danger of getting diabetes!'

'Oh, Annabelle,' laughs Nadia and then asks more soberly, 'how is Ralph?' Annabelle replies that her son is fine and confides that he's thinking of opening a computer business when he finishes college.

'Well,' says Nadia, glancing in the direction of the food table where one or two guests are helping themselves lavishly, 'there's a lot of money to be made in that.'

'Yes. Isn't there just?' says Annabelle, curtly tipping her head in Mo's direction.

'Mo used to play chess against computers,' says Nadia, trying to keep to the role of dutiful hostess.

'Really?' drawls Annabelle. She's bored. Menials are of no social significance and can be forgotten straight away.

'Where is everybody? Who's coming tonight?'

Nadia smiles with embarrassment. 'Why, everybody! Including Max, Paul, Lucretia, Philippa, Chris, myself and . . . Mo the gardener's here already.' She laughs.

They are already beginning to make Mo feel a little uneasy. More couples arrive and, after greeting each other loudly, help themselves to drinks. At first glance they all seem poorly dressed but a closer look shows it as a façade. Their clothes are expensive – although some of the men could do with a shave. Dodgy walking around like that, thinks Mo, two or three days' stubble on your face, dead cert for a tug. Forgetting for the moment that these people go round in cars.

Through the beat of the music Nadia catches the sound of the phone ringing in another room. That's bound to be Lucretia, she thinks as she goes to answer it. But when she picks up the phone it is not Lucretia's voice but Max's, informing her that Lucretia is feeling under the weather with a heavy cold and will not be able to make it. After putting down the phone Nadia goes in search of Mo, and bending over him tells him the news. Mo hesitates, his interest waning. If Lucretia isn't coming, he's going. Making the sudden resolve not to work for any more of these people, he starts to rise but Nadia, mistaking disinterest for indecision puts out a restraining hand, 'She's very nice, you know. Not as nice as me, of course,' she adds coyly, pushing back a strand of hair that has fallen over her face and modestly pulling the front of her blouse together where it has separated when she bent down.

This helps to appease Mo. Anyway, what harm will it do? he thinks. And besides (now that he is confronted), doesn't everybody dislike the boss?

'She's *so* witty. Always making jokes,' whispers Nadia. 'You'll like her. I'll give you her phone number.'

Mo thinks again. He has many reasons for refusing but they all seem to start from the wrong angle. His resolution breaks. Anyway, how is he to get his stuff typed without money?

'When shall I phone her?' he asks.

'In about a week,' replies Nadia, 'say next Saturday.'

123

'Right,' says Mo. Now he has accepted the job he feels relieved as it also affords him a genuine excuse to leave Nadia's employ. She can hardly expect him to keep working for them both. And, of course, he has to write as well.

Noting Mo's thoughtfulness Nadia pulls the front of her blouse closer together as she straightens up. But if 'modesty' is aimed at concealing rather than emphasising her breasts, the tautening of the material has the opposite effect, so that they jut out firmly on either side of her daintily clenched fist. Mo, trying for the best way to put things, does not even notice. 'I shan't be able to cut the grass for you any more this year,' he says slowly.

'Sorry?' says Nadia, looking at him.

'I shan't be able to cut the grass for you,' repeats Mo, explaining his reasons to her kindly.

Now the hand clutching the blouse gives the impression of anxiety. Mo, touched by her sad expression, begins to feel sorry for her. He is about to add that perhaps he can manage to come if not every week, then perhaps every second week, when some of the guests call Nadia from the other side of the room. 'Oh. It's quite all right,' says Nadia, bending nearer. 'There's far too much mess and rubbish in gardens nowadays.' An aggressive smell of garlic pierces Mo's nostrils as she leans further over him to whisper in his ear, 'so, I'm thinking of having it paved. Much more hygienic.'

In a country where superiority is measured by a cultured tone, the guests all converse in similar well-modulated voices. Not quite BBC, but it may just as well be. Mo begins to circulate, his formerly narrow slice of awareness expanding rapidly. He notes how frank discussions predominate among this intellectual gathering, and Mo concludes that this group by the bookcase earnestly supports social reform – in other countries – while that crowd by the fireplace show an eagerness for equality – in Ecuador. Although they drink heavily no one shows any sign of wanting to break into song.

He moves on. A man and a woman nearby are discussing a fringe play, Mark Lane and Sarah Stone, first-generation exiles from Highgate and Hampstead. They've started their own theatre company on Daddy's money, concealing along the way any link with Daddy. The woman's animated enthusiasm causes Mo to lean closer but they continue to ignore him. Mo gathers that the play has been written by the man while the woman, who must be his lover, is the director. He listens intrigued, hearing that the play is about the gruelling lives of the working classes. Sarah and Mark, while living off grants, are in the habit of going among the deprived, getting them to relate their stories, then dramatising them. Having gone to so much trouble to establish street credibility, it is lamentable to see that the only genuine thing about them is the gel they use to plaster down their hair. The firm that makes it seems to use real axle grease. With practised casualness they smile at Mo, covering their determination to exclude him from their conversation.

Hopefully, Mo continues to seek a friendly face among this shoal of cultured sharks. His perseverance is to be applauded. As he approaches the drinks table and is about to veer away, a man hails him. After the exchange of a few pleasantries it becomes apparent that he is in the company of a literary agent. Mo's heart lifts.

'Oh, you're like a boxing manager?' Mo exclaims. 'Are you a sort of talent scout?'

Overwhelmed by the bluntness of the question the man is caught off guard. 'Yes. I suppose I am.'

As Mo is about to carry on the conversation, Sophie pads by and is hailed desperately by the man. Mo's eyes light up at the sight of her again, as if she were an old and trusted friend. But she ignores him, pecking the man on the cheek instead. 'How are you, Chris? Haven't seen you for ages.' They immediately become engrossed in each other. Mo stands quietly, listening. He thinks he's offended her in some way. 'It's all so very complicated,' ends Sophie.

'But surely they all have the same language roots?' counters Chris.

'No, no, no,' corrects Sophie, with some heat. 'It's very hard to distinguish tribal accents.'

She's looking blankly at Mo when she says this. And taking it that it is to him she is speaking, he replies, 'I never knew that, but when Scotch Billy and Belfast Joe are drunk it's hard to distinguish between their accents.'

Sophie's eyes suddenly focus on Mo. Then, patting her mouth delicately to suppress a bored little yawn, she turns her face towards Chris. 'Such fiercely arrogant and proud people. But it's so hard to find real authenticity these days.' Chris nods understandingly. The conversation peters out as they move away. Mo finds himself on the edge of another conversation. This time two men of vastly differing ages are talking. Father and son? Lovers? Mo isn't sure.

'She had her own house. A ratepayer tried to make changes. Used her vote.'

'That'll do her a lot of good.'

'How many times have you done that, then?'

'What?'

'Voted.'

'Actually, I don't bother.'

'Leave it to others, do you?'

'Doesn't make much difference, one vote.'

'Where would the country be if everybody took that attitude?'

'Maybe a lot better off.'

'Don't you think local councils do enough?'

'I'm not sure.'

'There's no satisfying some. Look at the new swimming bath they've just opened.'

Mo jumps in at this point. 'Yes. Only trouble is, it's nearly always closed. Shut up shop when they feel like it. Breaks everybody's routine. Youngster turns up, can't get in. Wallop, turns to crime.'

They both look at him aghast. 'What a penetrating analysis. Our prisons overflowing, full to the brim, with thousands of frustrated swimmers,' says the older man.

As they speak a woman flops at Mo's feet. It's Annabelle. Sophie and Chris rush over.

'Perhaps she's just fainted. Maybe we could revive her,' says Sophie, loosening the top of Annabelle's dress. 'She has tremendous faith in alternative medicine. Swears by it.'

'It will take a bit more than homeopathy and aromatherapy to cure what she's suffering from now,' says Chris, looking at Mo.

Gathering that the matter is closed, Mo changes the subject. 'Do you know anything about getting stuff published?'

'I do indeed,' says Chris looking disdainfully at Mo. 'But there's nothing around worth publishing.'

Suddenly the music is turned up. Mo realises it is popular stuff. Street sounds. He'd expected this lot to be classical buffs, since they are the same in every other respect as the South Bank mob. Another man joins him. 'Hello, I'm Paul,' he says.

Their self-possession mixed with a shrill theatrical manner is beginning to unnerve Mo, making him unsure how to react. 'I'm Mo.' Paul seats himself beside Mo. He is a big-boned, wild-looking man in a dark checked sports jacket and an old pair of corduroy trousers. Playing at being destitute. Seems heedless but probably nobody's fool.

'I'm in publishing at the moment. What do you do?'

'I'm unemployed,' says Mo.

'Yes, there's a lot of it about,' quips Paul, taking a sip from his glass.

'Don't worry, it's not catching,' laughs Mo. Paul laughs too and asks Mo what he wants to drink.

Mo is beginning to dread this question. 'Nothing, thanks.' He squirms uncomfortably.

Annabelle has come round and is rallying herself in a chair. 'Why don't you have something to drink?'

'I don't want one, thanks.' The truth would take longer to explain.

'Why are you trying so hard to stay sober? Aren't you bored?' bulldozes Annabelle petulantly.

'No, I'm just trying to stay off the streets. It's hard to come back off the streets,' replies Mo thoughtfully.

'We drink. Drink won't harm anyone.'

127

'It's OK, but I don't want one.'

A chivalrous friend comes to Annabelle's assistance, filling her empty outstretched hand with a gin and tonic. 'I'm so tired,' she says. 'What do you do, Mo?'

'I'm out of work.'

She peeps over the top of her glass at him. 'Oh, that's terrible. What a shame.'

At this, Anton turns round submitting Mo to a searching glance.

'No, I don't mind,' says Mo in a low tone.

'But how boring,' says Annabelle, putting on what passes for a bored face. 'How do you fill in the time?'

'Well, I try to write a bit.' (The way they're knocking it back would put the lads in the park to shame, thinks Mo.)

'You?' says Annabelle, showing more than a little surprise.

'Yes. I've written a book and I'm working on another one.' He laughs. 'Looks like I'll have many more written before . . . I don't really know how to go about getting published.'

'What's your book about? Messing in the garden?' laughs Annabelle teasingly, finishing her drink.

Mo laughs too, then smiles at her. He likes her and her dress. But the other guys are not allowing themselves to be fascinated by see-through dresses. And the women are not allowing themselves to be fascinated by the men.

Under the influence of alcohol the women's rigidity is gradually being replaced by cocked-hipped sensuality. They remark how hard it is to find a man of forty who is not either gay or totally fucked up. It is not clear what they would do having found such a man, since they themselves seem continually on the verge of hysteria. Anyway, those with the prettiest noses will still get the best deals and the most aggressive will remain dominant.

'There's a beautiful moon tonight,' sighs Annabelle, ambling towards the window, pausing under the light to smile dreamily back at Mo. 'I'm under the influence of Taurus, you know.'

'I thought you were under the influence of something,' he laughs, shifting his seat for a better view.

The light does the rest. The vision is interrupted as Annabelle turns, making straight for him. Quite drunk now, she sits down, swinging her feet aggressively. 'What did you say you do?' she slurs.

Mo is beginning to get fed up with it all, wishing he hadn't stayed. But at first the word party had conjured up a certain magic. A fantasy in which one might even get to go home with Cinderella at twelve o'clock. But he hasn't got a watch.

'Nothing. I'm a dosser,' he replies.

'A what?'

'A dosser.'

'And what does a dosser do, darling?'

'Nothing, if he's a good one. He just dosses.'

'Where do you stay at night?'

'Up the convent with the Sisters of Mercy.'

Her head has dropped forward and she lifts it up abruptly. 'Yes. They'd need lots of mercy to look after some . . . Where do you sleep in the convent?'

'Beside the head nun's office.'

'You mother fucker!' she shrieks, laughing uproariously. Everyone turns slowly to gaze at Mo. He leans in conspiratorially.

'No. Mother Superior fucker,' he says quietly.

For answer, Annabelle lifts her legs and, banging her boots down near Mo, stares at him aggressively.

'You've got some unique foot movements,' he says, a little nervously.

She bursts out laughing at this. 'I like you. I like you. You shall come to work for me.' She looks at him flirtatiously. 'I've got a little job for you. Yes?'

'Yes. Straight away, if you like.' Mo needs no prompting but she's falling asleep and he wonders if she'll remember tomorrow.

He's thinking about leaving as she comes to. She tries

pulling a cross face at him but somehow it makes her look cute. 'What happened to your front teeth?' she darts at him suddenly.

Mo is surprised at her powers of recuperation. 'I was eating my dinner one night when they snapped.'

She seems shocked for a second, then, seeing Mo's amusement, replies, 'It must have been a tough dinner?'

'Not really,' he says, 'it was the salt.'

'The salt?' echoes Annabelle tipsily, with a quizzical laugh.

'Yes. It was a bit far away. As I reached for it my chest crushed up against the table. My teeth were in the inside pocket.' He glances at her but Annabelle, head drooped forward on to her chest, has conked out at last.

Paul and Nadia come over. 'Is she OK?' Nadia is pensive.

Mo looks at Annabelle. 'Yes. She's just having a little kip.'

They give a smile of relief. 'Well, Mo. Why didn't you tell me you were a writer?' asks Paul, already forgetting about Annabelle.

'I don't like to call myself a writer until I've been published.'

'What's your book about?'

'It's . . . sort of . . . about low life.'

Paul brightens instantly at this. 'Oh. You mean gangsters and criminals?' he asks, eyes flashing provocatively.

'No. More like dishwashers, rapists and winos,' says Mo quietly.

Paul turns. 'What an aura this man's got. So pure. So *simpático*,' he coos to Nadia.

'Why don't you make it charisma?' asks Mo drily.

'Oh, no. Charisma's down, aura's high.'

'Yes,' pipes Nadia, 'that's what attracted me to him the first time I met him. I should never have let anyone else put a hand on my lawn.'

Mo looks smug. 'Well, now that you two find me so attractive, how about a nice little job, writing or something? Instead of all this labouring work?'

130

'Now, now, Mo. You're not starving,' says Nadia, absent-mindedly looking at his empty plate.

'Yes. But you can't live off your aura. You can't pay the rent with it. Try it some time,' says Mo taking his last glance at Annabelle's sleeping form before rising to leave.

Anton has been studying Mo gravely for some time. Now he clears his throat before speaking. 'Mo. Why don't you come along to one of our meetings on Friday night?'

'What meetings are you talking about?' asks Mo, stopping in the middle of the room on his way to the door.

'Well . . . uh . . . I say meeting. It's an informal group really, where we get together to discuss our relationships and experiences.' He looks at the others to see if they are listening.

'No, thanks. I already go to the First of May group on Friday evenings.'

Anton shows interest at this. 'I've not heard of them. What do they do?'

Mo continued his walk towards the door. 'Well, every October as they experience winter's first cold,' he replies with mock seriousness, 'they all book into the nearest doss-house and they don't come back out again until it's warm enough to kip in the park.'

Tourists puzzle worriedly over journey planners, trailing brightly coloured rucksacks stuck over with badged emblems proclaiming countries visited en route. The train is overdue, platform crowded, passengers' necks craning towards the tunnel. A signal failure is announced and there will be delays. The voice on the Tannoy is pompous, as if doing travellers a favour. Mo squeezes himself against the wall, packed tight in the subdued waiting to ride the iron mile.

Hell Bent or Heaven Sent?

Commuters last night found themselves riding the Northern Line alongside the British Brigade of the New York vigilante group Guardian Angels. The police have said that the Angels' distinctive studded arm-bands and insignia-infested red berets could be classed as offensive weapons as they swagger about their self-appointed task of clearing up the subway.

Mo struggles to hold his position as the waiting masses swell, buffeting and battering his paper. He found safe anchorage between two corpulent commuters, realigning against a third's substantial back. Averting his gaze to the article, he found his place with a sigh.

It may seem ironic that a group of poor, mostly black ghetto dwellers, and young middle-class whites, should be making the tubes safe for the affluent culture hawks of the South Bank, and can be hired for no more than the price of a bit of publicity and a few free dinners, to protect the property of the haves from the have-nots.

Grub and aggrandisement! thinks Mo wryly as he continues to read.

> But their main claim to fame here at present seems to be their ability to run up two lengths of escalator without needing artificial respiration afterwards. They are known in America as the Pussy Posse, on account of their leader being a woman. Asked his opinion of the Angels a sergeant commented, 'A gang of petty thugs and twilight types, turned into the martial arm of the middle classes. Won't be long before they are using dosshouse rejects and re-habbed druggies to do their dirty work . . .

Another swell sinks Mo's paper and he gives up trying to read.

Old Tommy the Leaf stirs. Teasy Jeannie twists, the damp heat exploding in her crotch. A pleasant warmth pervades sleep, spreading slowly down her thighs. It takes a while for her mind to convey what her body feels. She wakes as the warm liquid continues to flow down her legs and forms a puddle on the floor where she lies. She sits up, easing her back against the wall, searching her pockets, desperate as the soggy fag butts crumble in her hand. 'Is that you, Tommy?' she calls, eyes squinting to focus.

'Yeah, it's me.' A barrage of racking coughs shatter the silence. The stale smell of human shit and urine hang in the air. The windows of the room have been boarded up by the council. The odour cannot escape. Broken chairs and other furniture discarded by the previous occupants make it difficult in the absence of light to move around without bashing a limb. The house, like its two occupants, is on the verge of collapse.

'Have you got a smoke on yer, Tommy?' croaks Jeannie. The pee drying into her buttocks and thighs saps her vitality. A wave of sickness sweeps over Tommy as he fumbles to light the butt he's found. Quick drags bring the blood rushing to his head. He passes the butt to Jeannie's outstretched hands. The fag takes her mind off her discomfort, until Tommy, struggling to rise, falls down, going into convulsions, jerking, shaking, frothing.

'Jesus!' screams Jeannie, the butt burning her fingers as she fights to save Tommy from smashing his head.

It ends as quickly as it began. Her pity becomes tinged with envy as she watches him breathing. She must get the price of a drink. She looks at his face, calm and peaceful, calculating the odds of him waking if she were to dip him. Only the most depraved punters pay to hump through folds of smelly piss. No jerking or fumbling, her hand slides down his pockets with practised ease, and comes back up with nothing. A spiteful reminder of her plight. She must get a change of clothes. But where? Charity, it seems, no longer begins at home. Oxfam? No good, even with a pound or two, since the well-off's whimsical flirtations with fashion have turned a shop-for-the-needy into a shop-for-the-greedy.

The nagging question: how to get drink? Tommy's face looks more calm, content, handsome even, thinks Jeannie, as she bends over him to open the waistband of his trousers and fly. Every now and then she stops her dreamy fumblings to check he's still asleep before going back to pull at the trousers, which have become wedged between his body and the floor. Tommy never stirs as she pulls them off. That fit, she thinks, sitting back on her haunches, resting from the effort of it all, was double bad. Still watching Tommy, she takes off her shabby skirt, torn knickers and laddered tights.

The office workers rush on by. Males with briefcases in bowlers and pinstripes. Secretaries, some with little slave chains on their ankles. Beautiful birds, brilliant plumage. Laura was a secretary once but reckons she has a bone disease. This gives her face, depending on where you stand to view it, either a malformed look or an attractive slant. What with this and the endearing little habit she's developed of sniffing Tippex fumes, is it any wonder she took to the bottle, finally ending on the streets?

Laura watches her come through the station door. Jeannie seems different today. It takes a moment to realise why; then she smiles at the trousers knowingly. Unable to make any money in the time-honoured way herself, it being the wrong time of the month, she is to be doubly disappointed. Jeannie is without funds. As Jeannie joins her on the bench they go into a huddle of vague gestures, signs, odd words. Anyone listening would have been none the wiser to what is passing between them.

Deprivation scours all those whose features it touches in much the same way. But in Laura's case it is etched so delicately that strangers, seeing her for the first time, often mistake her for someone who's suffered a tropical disease, or fallen on hard times. What a boon! Whether Laura knows it or not this is the only reason she draws hardly a stray glance, never mind suspicious look, in the Ladies' Room, where she is often to be found, sitting in the best vantage point by the door waiting to swoop on the first careless traveller's bag.

The trousers are a size too small and Jeannie's arse wobbles as she walks. It only takes two turns of the station before a punter, deciding she's rear-of-the-year, moves in. On that beam of sex she takes in his shoulders and chest. He doesn't haggle the price as he follows her out.

The hallway of the skipper is gloomy and dark. They begin kissing. A breeze ripples. He thinks he hears a noise. But Jeannie clasps him tighter. After that he hesitates no longer and begins to float with her tongue down his throat. Sigh. Die. As his hand touches her thigh, light explodes in his head. In that moment he must have weighed a ton, flopping forward heavily. As he slides down Jeannie's body, unconscious, to the floor, Laura, bending swiftly, drops the empty cider bottle to relieve him of his wallet, his ring . . . everything. The day is brightening up as they sidle back on to the street.

Edinburgh Ann seems overdressed. The sun at its highest and she's wearing a brand new gentleman's overcoat a size too large. But, then, she's not had much choice in its purchase, speed being the essence of the disc-swapping caper at which Ann makes her living. Visiting the best shops armed with a small bolt cutter to snip the security discs from coats, she pops the disc into another shopper's bag. When Security jumps on the stooge, buzzer ringing at the door, Ann's out the other with the coat.

Jeannie and Laura spot her as they turn the corner with the carry-out. Jealousy being the same whether it's manifested in the lounge of the nearest five-star or in the gutter, they both cross to the opposite side of the street. The manoeuvre doesn't escape Ann, though her back is half turned.

'Sod her,' says Jeannie as they reach the other side. 'Her and her fancy clothes. She's no' getting any drink off me today.' They pass with embarrassed smiles. Ann, giving a curt nod, busies herself checking up and down the street for the buyer. Her heart lifts. Is that Shuffling Eric, the fence's runner, at last? She squints painfully, trying, with impotent fumings, to will him into focus. Eyes shielded, unsure. It must be Eric. As he draws nearer Ann's face undergoes a rapid change. Tommy hobbles up, face creased with stress, clad in a tattered jacket and Jeannie's old skirt. Nose welded dry by blood and snot, frustrated every time he attempts speech, she screeches with laughter. At last Tommy manages to catch a breath long enough to explain. He'd woken alone in the skipper with no recollection of what had happened. Ann strips her teeth in a grim smile. What a mess.

Tommy, exhausted by the effort, leans back against a concrete post. 'There's drink around, Ann. Nose Job just met Jeannie and Laura coming out of the off-licence with an armful of bottles.' He lowers his voice. 'I heard they just rolled a businessman.'

Pity? Perhaps. Or is another idea forming in her head? Whatever, Ann is now in trouble, neither the fence nor his runner having shown. To top it all she's beginning to get the shakes. 'Here, Tommy,' she says, taking off the coat with a flourish, 'put this round you.' Tommy, jumping at the chance to cover his embarrassment, wrestles himself into it, calling all the saints to witness the good deed. 'Aye, Tommy,' she says, motioning. 'Take off that stupid skirt.' Turning sideways on he buttons the coat around, letting the skirt fall to the ground. Stepping out of it, he lifts his foot contemptuously to kick it into the road. Ann's voice stops him. 'No!' she says, bending to retrieve it. 'Never know when I'll need a change,' she adds, in answer to Tommy's quizzical look. Skirt and women being synonymous, no further explanation is needed.

And so they part, Tommy, unencumbered, heading swiftly for the station, Ann moving off towards the park. She glimpses them seated close together on the steps of a derelict house, bottles of wine at their feet. They've certainly seen Ann coming, but do not look up, chortling instead at some unheard joke. Ann hesitates, nervous before the two lounging in the sun, looking at Laura as if asking her to note her patience before speaking. 'The law's after a couple of women that mugged a guy near the station earlier on.'

'So?' replies Jeannie and Laura with more than a little aggression.

'So . . . one of them was wearing trousers,' replies Ann. And taking Jeannie's folded skirt from under her arm she holds it out. All pretext drops as Jeannie takes the drying skirt.

'Keep your eyes peeled while I change,' she says, her movements feverish and jerky. She gives a nod to the bottles on the floor. 'Get stuck in.'

With a surge of relief Ann lifts the bottle to her mouth, swallowing the magic fluid quickly to ease her nerves and banish the shakes. She tries to judge how long it will be before the law really gets round to looking, making a mental note to blow as soon as she gets the glow.

As he walks out of the station where they've arranged to meet, she is leaning against a wall eating a sandwich. 'Are you Mo?' she says, eyeing him sharply. He's looking into two big beautiful brown eyes. She has short stylish black hair and a slightly olive complexion. 'I'm Lucretia.' It isn't a greeting, it's an edict, a proclamation from Caesar's wife.

'Yes.'

'I'm sorry. I've got to eat this now. I'm too busy to stop. Have you had something to eat?' she asks.

'Yes, thanks.'

'Good, my car's over there.'

Walking beside her, Mo realises she's tall. 'If I keep my back straight, I'll be as tall.' Watch it, Mo. She's already getting you on your toes! Mo judges her to be about thirty-five though she has the figure of a young girl.

They reach the car. She gets in. Mo tries his side. It's open.

'I don't bother locking it,' she says tersely. Fastening her seat-belt she starts the engine and off they drive.

Mo is trying to weigh her up and forgets to put on his own seat-belt. He feels silly doing it up later. 'Oh, you don't remind anyone to put their belt on. It's them who get nicked now, not the driver,' he says, with floundering embarrassment.

'Yes,' she replies, laughing. She couldn't care less if her passengers went right through the windscreen.

The first thing Mo notices when he gets out of the car is that Lucretia's house is much larger than Nadia's. 'It's far too big for us,' she says, sensing Mo's thought. Not knowing how many are included in the 'us', Mo gives what he hopes will pass for an understanding smile, trailing behind her as she leads the way through the front door along a hallway into a large, expensively furnished front room.

139

'I hope you're feeling strong today,' says Lucretia, taking off her coat and continuing without waiting for Mo's reply, 'because I want that tree cut down.'

Mo glances through the sliding glass doors at a sturdy, virile-looking tree. 'It's a nice big healthy tree, that,' says Mo.

'I'm sure it is,' replies Lucretia curtly, eyeing Mo as if seeing him for the first time. 'Nature's fine, until it starts interfering with the light.'

'Yes, it is a bit dark and gloomy in here,' muses Mo, without choosing his words. But Lucretia, lost in thought, does not appear to notice.

'Have you got an axe and a saw?' asks Mo, sliding the doors apart.

'Yes, wait,' says Lucretia, opening a side door and calling out. 'Max!'

'Hello,' replies a man's voice.

'Can you come and get the garden tools for us?' A medium-built, affable-looking man comes into the room. 'Will you show Mo where the tools are?' says Lucretia, combining introduction with order.

After leaving Mo in the garden, Max returns to the living room where Lucretia is sifting through the pages of a magazine. 'Max, did you insert the ad for the picket?' asks Lucretia.

'Yes, it's in there somewhere,' he says.

Lucretia locates it and begins to read. After a few minutes she looks back up at Max. 'There's certainly going to be quite a turnout.'

'Yes,' replies Max, 'it's about time we took action against Blyton and her ilk instead of just talking about it.'

Lucretia gives an involuntary shudder. 'A complete and utter pain. Such pedantic prose. Unlimited amounts of ginger beer and freshly baked cakes. And the smiling submission of all those feudal villagers . . .' Her eyes glint aggressively. 'We shall be making a very positive statement against all that middle-class hogwash on Saturday next.'

'Talking about statements,' says Max, 'I'd like to state

140

here and now that I'd like this room free on Tuesday night as I'm meeting Peter for the first time.'

'Impossible,' cries Lucretia, 'I've got a meeting here on Tuesday night.'

'Can't you take them upstairs?'

'Hardly. Some of them are heavily pregnant.'

At this Max gives a surprised, 'Oh.'

As they speak piano music drifts into the room. 'What's Philippa doing at that piano? She's supposed to have flu. That's why I've let her stay home from school,' says Lucretia, shaking her head in exasperation. 'Are you going in today, Max?'

'Got to,' he answers, picking up some typing paper and joining her at the table.

'Has Mo started on that tree yet?' asks Lucretia.

'Yes, I've shown him what to do. By the way, where's he been working?'

'I really don't know,' says Lucretia, thumbing through the magazine, 'but Nadia thinks he spent some time in prison.'

'Really? Joe's doing an article on prisons, perhaps I should have a chat with him.'

'There's no rush. He should be here for a while. I've got quite a bit for him to do. He seems very friendly, and also very reasonable. He only charges £2 an hour.'

'A true socialist,' grins Max.

As he speaks the tree Mo has been sawing suddenly crashes to the ground, some of its branches landing half-way through the open glass doors. They jump to their feet with shock as Mo enters, axe in hand.

'Oh, you must be gentle,' flutters Lucretia, 'I must have gentle people around me.'

'Sorry,' Mo apologises breathlessly.

Max makes for the hall door. 'I'll leave you to it,' he hurls back as he leaves.

Mo grasps a branch of the tree, trying, with brute force, to drag it back out through the doors. He pulls and wrenches, but it has become wedged fast.

'My goodness, what are you doing? You're like Attila the

Hun. Wait, let me,' says Lucretia, bending to lift one of the branches, a heavy grunt showing it's too much for her.

Suddenly the end Mo is tugging gives. He lifts it clean up in the air, in the same motion throwing it back out through the door.

'You're very strong,' says Lucretia, 'but you don't look it. Now you must get on. Cut it all up,' she continues, bustling around, picking up the odd twig here and there. Mo smiles. 'Yes,' she goes on, 'cut it small, and keep all the pieces. They're very good for barbecue fires.'

'Have you got a smaller saw?' asks Mo, looking at the scattered branches.

'Yes,' says Lucretia, opening a cupboard and reaching inside. Straightening up she hands him a miniature saw.

Mo looks at it, amused. 'This won't be much good. It's for cutting metal.'

Lucretia wrings her hands. 'Of course it will. Oh dear, if I had the time I'd do it myself in half an hour.'

'What with – your nail file?'

Lucretia looks at him. 'Are we being silly?'

Mo shrugs and goes back out to the garden.

Lucretia glances out of the window as she goes to answer the phone. She watches for a second, noting the flowing motion with which Mo manoeuvres. She picks up the phone. 'Hello. Yes.' She listens for a while to the voice at the other end. 'OK, thanks for phoning. 'Bye, Rosa.'

Just then Mo comes back into the room, asking for a drink of water.

'Of course,' she says, looking at him thoughtfully. 'Help yourself. You know, when I first saw you, Mo, I thought you were a gipsy. You're not a gipsy, are you?'

'No,' says Mo, a little surprised.

They look at each other silently.

'There's nothing wrong with gipsies. One asked me out once, but I never went,' she sighed.

Mo finishes his drink slowly, feigning disinterest. He's become much more self-confident since working for Nadia. 'You know,' he begins, 'I won't be able to cut that tree up without some help.'

The combination of his calm resolve, and the size of the tree, sways her, 'OK,' she said. 'Do you know someone, then?'

Mo replaces the cup. 'I did. Old Kelly used to help me with sawing up trees. It made it a lot easier to have someone pushing the other end.'

'Where does he live? Can't you get in touch with him?' she asks quickly.

'No, he's homeless. Used to sleep by the dustbins in a council block, until the caretaker got to know about it.'

'Well, what is he doing now, then?'

Mo shrugs. 'Oh, a bit of this, a bit of that. You know how it is.'

'No, I don't know how it is. What exactly do you mean? Does he not wish to help you any more?' Lucretia is growing impatient.

Mo shakes his head sadly. 'He can't. He's helping other people now.'

'Oh. Who is he helping?'

'The police.'

'The police?' echoes Lucretia. 'How is he helping them?'

'With inquiries.'

She bursts out laughing. 'Well, I hope they find him satisfactory.'

'I'm sure they will,' says Mo.

'Well, you will have to get someone quickly to help you with that tree. I haven't got anything else for you to do until that mess is cleared up.' Her eyes light on the wall. 'Unless you can construct a series of wooden shelves for me. Do you know anything about woodwork?' Mo shakes his head negatively as Lucretia stares at him. 'Well, no matter, it's quite easy really. And I'll help you.' Mo brightens up as Lucretia produces a large sheet of drawing paper. 'Now, look at this drawing. Read it.'

Mo looks at it for a long while in silence. Lucretia taps her foot on the floor. She is becoming irritable with Mo's inability to understand it. 'I don't get it,' says Mo, puzzled by all the lines and graphs.

'Yet it's clear enough,' announces Lucretia bossily.

Mo shakes his head again. 'It is to you, perhaps, but, then, you've got the idea in your head and I haven't.'

'Even for a gardener you seem unusually dense,' she sighs. 'Why do I have to do everything?' she asks in a tone of martyred despair. 'It's always the same. When you ask a man to cook dinner, nine times out of ten he'll keep pestering you for the pepper and salt.'

'But I don't know anything about woodwork . . . or gardening for that matter.'

Lucretia looks straight at him with sarcasm. 'Well, what do you know about, for heaven's sake?' she asks acidly.

'Writing,' says Mo shyly. 'I try to write. I've nearly finished my second book. I'm trying to get a publisher. That's why I do these odd labouring jobs, so I can afford to get my stuff typed.'

She laughs. 'How quaint. An author in labour!'

Mo is visibly peeved by this. 'Perhaps you'd be better off with a professional?'

'No,' says Lucretia, firmly. 'They wanted £100 to do the job . . . and they'd trample all my herbs down. But I'll stay with you, so you don't do the same.'

'I don't know if I can do it, really,' says Mo, with waning enthusiasm.

Turning suddenly, Lucretia knocks the drawing off the table. As she squats down to pick it up her skirt gapes open at the front, revealing brown woollen stockings that end half-way up her thighs. Gathering the drawing up with one hand while balancing herself with the other, she smiles up at Mo. 'Don't you want to help me?' Mo is smitten and, unable to drag his eyes away from the delightful distraction, nods. 'Good. And Max shall help you with your book,' she replies, seeking to placate him.

'Terrific,' shouts Mo happily. 'I've got the manuscript with me. Have you got time for a quick look?'

'Yes. Let me see it.'

Mo grabs his jacket from the chair, pulling from it a bulky sheaf of papers encased in a blue folder. Lucretia takes them from him and starts to read while Mo resumes looking at her drawing.

After a while Lucretia looks up. 'Yes. It's good. It holds me. I'll speak to Max about getting it published.'

'Thank you,' says Mo, overjoyed by her apparent appreciation of his writing.

'OK. I'll put it where it will be safe,' she says, leaving it on the table.

After a cup of tea they begin work together on the shelves. This calls for more assistance than Lucretia has anticipated. 'I'm getting bored,' she remarks, after half an hour has passed.

'I'm going as fast as I can,' replies Mo, trying to screw a strut to an awkward wall angle. But Lucretia is not to be reasoned with.

'What are you messing around for?' she chides him.

Mo looks as if he's been slapped. Surely the matter is self-evident? 'I don't want this rough edge to cut someone,' he says quietly.

'Oh, leave it,' she says. 'If they tear their clothes it's their own fault.'

'That's not very nice, Lucretia,' says Mo, rubbing it down speedily.

'Oh. Do you do everything fast?' she hisses spitefully.

Mo looks sad. 'We don't seem to hit it off very well,' he says. She looks at him with surprise as he continues, 'You really might be better off with a professional.'

'No. I want to get these shelves up quickly,' she replies in a coaxing tone. 'Professionals make a lot of noise.' She pauses. 'Yes, far too much noise. And fuss. One has to keep handing them cups of tea, coffee. Pandering to their every whim. Not like my big strong clever writer.'

Although this seems to appease him, Mo still decides to stop work. 'Well, I think I'll just finish up for today,' he says.

'What would I do without you,' purrs Lucretia.

'OK, I'll see you tomorrow, then,' says Mo, smiling as he finishes what he is doing. 'And I'll try to get one of my mates along to help me with the tree.'

'That'll be splendid, Mo,' says Lucretia warmly, handing

him a key. 'In case I'm not in when you get here. Oh, and by the way, can you start earlier tomorrow?'

'I'll try,' says Mo, pulling the door closed behind him.

Mo knocks on the basement door. Getting no answer he lets himself in with the key. The cat is pacing the kitchen floor, stiff-tailed and angry. Mo hears the gurgling slurp of water flowing down a pipe when the plug is pulled.

'Is that you, Mo?' calls Lucretia from the bathroom.

'Yes,' he answers as she emerges, buttoning her dress. Mo hears a piano being played in another room. The cat springs up on to the settee. Settling down it starts to wash itself. Mo picks up a ruler and begins measuring a length of wood. Satisfied that it will fit he begins drilling the wall. 'Your daughter plays the piano very nicely,' he remarks, adjusting the shelf.

'My daughter plays with the piano,' shrugs Lucretia indifferently, struggling into her coat. 'That cat is hungry, I must go and get him some food at the corner shop.' She looks at the empty milk bottles cluttering the floor by the fridge. 'Could you put those bottles outside for me, please, Mo? I'm so rushed today.'

Slowly he puts down the screwdriver, gathers up half a dozen bottles in his arms and, following her towards the door, nearly collides with her back when she stops suddenly. Lifting her dress with a rustle and swish to adjust her petticoat, smiling cheekily over her shoulder, 'Sorry. It's so cold. I need all my folds today.'

Struggling to avoid mistaking the situation, Mo stands staring, trying to shape a face-saving sentence. As Lucretia disappears through the door he thinks of many good replies. But by then the moment has passed.

When Mo returns after leaving the bottles outside he finds a young girl, back facing him, standing by the electric cooker fiddling with the taps. She turns at his 'Hello'. Her thin child's body gives her a fragile look, but her nose, a little too bulbous, robs her face of any childlike quality. If it hadn't been for the wide-spaced brown eyes staring out

146

at him vacantly, seemingly sightless, he would never have taken her for Lucretia's daughter.

'Lucretia's gone to get some cat food,' says Mo by way of breaking the ice.

'Oh. Thank you,' replies Philippa, gently bending to pick up the cat in her rather large hands. Her short sausage-thick little fingers belie her musical sensitivity.

'I'd better get on with these shelves,' says Mo, making himself busy since Philippa seems preoccupied with stroking the cat.

'Oh, no!' says Philippa as Mo goes back to his work. Her voice startles him. He turns just in time to see the cat disappearing through a gap in the door that he's left ajar. Philippa springs after it with Mo close behind. Once outside, the cat slows down and begins an imaginary stalk at the foot of a low wall that runs alongside the garage. Seizing on the idea of driving the cat into a corner, Mo quickly spreads his arms and bending low, creeps slowly forward, shooing the cat before him.

'Watch out. He'll get past you,' shouts Philippa in excitement at being so near. As if at her words the cat suddenly turns, springing effortlessly between them to run back into the house.

'Quick!' cries Philippa, doubling back inside, followed by Mo.

'I nearly caught him out there,' says Mo, laughing.

Philippa, breathless with the game, pays him no heed. Instead, lunging at the door, she closes it with a bang. The next instant it flies back open as Lucretia steps through it, shouting, 'I'm back!' And in the same breath, 'Philippa, if you've got any washing to be done, fetch it down now.'

Apparently ignoring her, Philippa picks up the cat, singing to herself as she strokes him, 'Hitler has only got one ball. The other's in the Albert Hall . . .' Lucretia springs round, obviously aggravated. Mo's presence does not appear to inhibit either of them. Philippa continues tauntingly, '. . . and poor pussy's got no balls at all.'

'Are we being silly again?' screams Lucretia. 'Put that cat down and go and fetch your washing now!' But Philippa has no need to put the cat down. At Lucretia's scream it jumped from her grasp, landing on all fours by the fridge.

Looking straight ahead, Philippa walks silently towards the door. Lucretia glances at Mo, a little embarrassed. 'She's so bold,' she grins, 'it's the Continental blood in her. Makes her sulky. Ha ha ha.'

Philippa turns as she goes through the hall door. 'Anyone would be sulky with a mother like you,' she shouts back.

Lucretia laughs teasingly, still looking at Mo, who has stopped what he was doing to ask, 'Is Philippa's eyesight limited, then?'

'No,' snaps Lucretia. 'It's her understanding of biology that's limited.'

'I see,' says Mo. But he doesn't see immediately. It takes a little time to fathom what she meant. Then he feels uncomfortable and begins to busy himself with his work, mindful of a loud, angry, metallic purr as Lucretia, putting out some milk for the cat, slams the fridge door.

It is some time before Lucretia, having done a few chores about the house, and dealt with one or two phone-in clients, calls him over to the table where she has left him a croissant and a mug of tea. As he's finishing his tea Max comes in brandishing some papers.

Lucretia pushes her chair away from the table, taking the papers from him as she stands up. 'Why do I have to work so hard for so little money?' she asks jokingly. No one answers her. 'Because I do work very hard for it,' she continues, an annoyed look on her face as she throws the papers on to the table. Mo looks into his mug of tea. Max, without making any comment, walks out of the room whistling to himself.

When he's finished his tea, Mo returns to the shelves where he is trying to level an awkward wall angle while Lucretia, who is drying her hands after washing up, makes some approving remarks on the work, adding, in a sudden spasm of generosity, 'Mo. You came early today, so I'll pay you for four hours.'

Mo smiles at her. 'I only worked three and a half,' he says pleasantly. 'It doesn't really matter.'

'It matters to me,' she replies shrilly, waving some money at him which she has taken from her purse. Mo's embarrassment shows as he takes the money from her. He is slowly falling in love. It's quite touching, really. May be the most touching thing she's seen all week. But it's getting rather late, there's a lot of shopping to be done and loading it could be a trial with the traffic piling up behind. Perhaps without even realising it Lucretia takes advantage of his affection. 'Mo,' she begins, 'perhaps I could drop you off?' Before he can reply she thrusts a shopping bag in his hand, continuing quickly, 'I've got a little shopping to do first. Perhaps you could help me.' Mo nods at her gently. It's nearly like a date. He gets a warm feeling in his stomach. Can this be the turning point in his life?

In his room not even the movement of the pen can be heard as Mo begins to write. The reason for this is the noise below. It is deafening. 'They're off their fucking heads with drink again,' says Mo to himself angrily. Perhaps if he could come up with some inspiration he wouldn't feel so bad. His assumed date turned out to be a two-hour stress-inducing shopping trip and he was slowly beginning to make the grim connection between his previous prison work and drink record and his current severely limited choice in employment prospects. Further complications arise in his heart and mind when he remembers Lucretia. To neutralise them he thinks of the job. He'll have to go out to find Finn. Search the station. Yes, even go into the pub. And then what? He makes his way cautiously down the stairs past O'Neill's room where someone is threatening to kill someone else.

The train has just pulled to a stop as Mo sits waiting, sipping a can of lemonade on the platform seat. In the subdued neon lighting it seems like one of those posh restaurants. The type with walls of glass and fish swimming around inside . . . only it's people down here and they can't even move. Never mind swim. Flattened up against the glass of the tube doors, wedged so tight they look like dummies in a window display.

Before the doors are fully opened the passengers start to spill on to the platform, forcibly ejected by their travelling companions behind. Over the sound of this mêlée voices can be heard. Not the restrained buzz of commuter complaints but a nastier verbiage: predatory and menacing, verging on hysteria.

Three blacks surrounding a middle-aged white office

worker are pulling and tugging at him, demanding an answer to their questions. 'What you call me, man? You tell me. You say that again.' The impression other passengers get from this little encounter is that the blacks have somehow been maligned. Well, nobody likes to be insulted. Isn't a little indignation justified when perhaps it will all blow over as quickly as it began?

The man stands his ground, attempting several times to make himself clear, all to no avail. Desperately he appeals to the crowd. A few of the braver ones try to intervene but the blacks thwart each succeeding intercession, alienating him further from the crowd. Those that weren't nervous before are certainly nervous now. A delicate situation all round.

Mo takes another hit from his can. *Déjà vu*. Incidents differ but the best formulas stay the same: time to be about one's own business. The crowd begins to disperse. Oddly enough this is the very thing the three blacks had dreaded, for with the outer layers peeling back those remaining get a good clear look into the core of the matter. Far from making themselves scarce after their clumsily bungled effort at pickpocketing, they begin to rain blows on the abandoned traveller's face, while maniacally continuing to demand why he has bad-mouthed them. Suddenly the tallest of the three grasps the man by the lapels. Angling his body, dreadlocks swirling under his baker-boy's cap, he brings his knee up with vicious force into the traveller's groin. Somehow he still keeps his feet unable to retreat or to distinguish the difference between being right and pseudo-fight. He is also unable to see the wisdom of falling down so they hit him again and again until he does. As the man hits the ground they take pot luck with his briefcase. Mo takes off in the opposite direction.

Mo recognises the old scent immediately he opens the pub door. Finn is sitting in the corner. Holding court. Surrounded by some younger soccer fans to whom he is explaining his theses and theorems, and how the working class has the right to exploit their strength, although personally he didn't want to fight. But he wouldn't say no to a drink. He's pleased to see Mo. Especially when Mo puts one down in front of him. No Italian red tonight. Yes. Of course he'll be OK. 'See you in the morning.'

It's going to be a scorcher, thinks Mo, as he waits outside the station for Finn. Everything's arse upwards. Eight o'clock in the morning and the sun hot as hell. The one good day in the year, or maybe twenty years, it's happened, and we've got a fucking great oak tree to chop up. Lack of sleep has made him a bit irritable: he's not had much, with the noise below.

Just then Finn appears, his clothes twisted and crumpled, his once white shirt black with grime. Well, at least I've got a room and a bed, thinks Mo as he greets Finn, who is obviously suffering the effects of a hard night's skippering after leaving the pub.

'So what's she like, then?' growls Finn as they make for Lucretia's house.

'She's OK,' says Mo.

'Yeah . . . but?' probes Finn.

'You'll get a tenner out of it,' says Mo quickly, knowing that will stop Finn's inquisitiveness. He doesn't really know how to explain people like Lucretia in any understandable way to his former fellow vagrants. As they turn into Lucretia's pathway Mo, fearful that Finn might blow it, whispers, 'Don't nick anything here, and try to keep the verbal down to—'

'A scream,' interrupts Finn maliciously.

But even though he appears to be treating the job lightly he stops Mo a few steps from the door, putting his hand up warningly as he starts to take off his jacket with a conspiratorial wink. It is the work of a moment for a practised hand like Finn to complete his instant dry cleaning. He looks a new man as he waits with Mo for the door to be opened to their ring, in his inside-out shirt.

'Good. You've arrived at last,' says Lucretia, opening the door with a scowl.

'Hello,' says Finn, unnecessarily loudly, in an effort to

155

avoid being intimidated by her manner as she ushers them briskly through to the garden. Carefully explaining once again to Mo what needs to be done and with a look that says 'see that you get it done', she disappears back into the house as they go to get the tools from the shed.

Armed with a couple of axes and a two-handed saw, they set about severing the branches from the trunk. As they work Mo can't help noticing how double-glazed Finn's eyes have become. And the way his body shakes and trembles each time his axe misses, or bites too deep. Mo feels sorry for him, thinking of the heat, yet still hopes Finn will make it through the day, considering the work.

'It's a bastard,' says Finn loudly. He means to be heard.

Mo experiences a pang of guilt as he tells him to keep his voice down, remembering what it's like to be sick from drink. Even so, he still wishes Finn would change the subject. Or, better still, keep quiet altogether.

'OK. I'm going for a shit then,' says Finn angrily, throwing down his axe and wandering off, without even troubling to enquire where he needs to go. An image of a notice in an office flashes through Mo's mind: 'Beware the Walking Thief'.

Fuck him, if he goes on the creep here, thinks Mo dejectedly. He'll spoil it for me.

The smell of cooking, mingling with the sap of the freshly cut branches, causes Mo to look up. Lucretia is coming towards him with a tray. 'Here we are. Try some of this carrot cake,' she says, adding with a self-conscious smile, 'I hope you like it. It's home made.'

'It's delicious,' says Mo, after he's taken a bite.

'Good. And this is for your friend. By the way, where is he?' she asks, looking round.

'I'm here,' replies Finn, striding down the garden. 'Just been to the toilet.'

'There,' says Lucretia, pointing to where she's left the tray resting on the edge of the tree. 'Have a piece of cake, Mr . . . er . . . ?'

'Just call me Finn. Everyone else does,' says Finn, with a self-assured shrug.

He's nearly back to his old self again, thinks Mo, pleased by the prospect of not having to carry him through the rest of the work or the day.

'Well, then, have a piece of cake, Finn,' repeats Lucretia, this time picking up the tray and waving it so that it keeps touching his chest.

'What a pity. What a shame,' says Finn, pushing the tray away as gently as he can. 'I'm either blessed or cursed with a small appetite. Can't do justice to your cooking, I'm afraid . . . I'll take a drink of orange, though.' And with that he politely grasps the glass, swallowing greedily.

'Are you sure you can't eat it?' asks Lucretia, just as politely.

'No. Sorry,' blurts Finn as some of the liquid takes the wrong turning down his throat. 'Not the best way to endear yourself to the cook, I suppose,' he splutters.

'OK. Give it to me. I'm always hungry since I gave up smoking . . . I'll get fat,' says Lucretia hastily.

Finn looks at her admiringly. 'You'll never get fat. You've got a naturally trim figure.'

Lucretia bristles. 'What do you mean?' she asks, holding his glance with an annoyed look. 'You like women cute and helpless, do you?'

'I wish I'd kept my mouth shut,' says Finn gruffly.

'Yes. But the only time you seem to manage that is when you're offered something to eat,' she snaps, her politeness fading out completely.

Finn turns away as she walks back across the garden, stumbling slightly on some debris clustered near the back door.

'See. They're earth mother types,' says Mo, trying to be loyal, spreading wide his arms as if to demonstrate to Finn her healing energy. 'She's highly strung. All middle-class women are like that. They're a bit eccentric too,' he adds, taking a swipe at a branch. 'Don't like to see toilet seats left up. You know. Silly things like that, Finny.'

Finn doesn't answer. Instead he brings down his axe with such force that it cuts clean through a thick branch in one stroke. When Finn still doesn't answer, Mo goes on in an effort to humour him. 'You'd laugh if I told you about the last woman I was working for.' He leans on the tree, smiling at the memory of it. 'Some of the things she used to come out with!'

But Finn, not restricted by such considerations, bends down, picks up a branch and throwing it on to the pile, mumbles, 'Guilt-ridden bastards.'

'What?' queries Mo.

'Guilt-ridden middle-class bastards,' repeats Finn. 'I've met her type before. What a stroppy cow!' he goes on, grabbing at his jacket in an impulse of fury and pulling from his inside pocket a three-quarters-full bottle of cooking wine. Wrenching off the cork, he raises it to his lips. It happens so suddenly that for a few seconds Mo is stunned for want of words and what to do.

'Here,' says Finn, proffering the bottle to Mo, who has suddenly planted himself between Finn and the house. 'Have a slug.'

'No. No,' says Mo, recoiling in horror from the out-stretched bottle in Finn's hand. 'You shouldn't have took it, Finny. You're going to drop me in it.'

'Sod it,' says Finn, by way of excuse, raising the bottle to his mouth once more. 'I had to have a cure.'

Nearly overcome by the impossibility of the situation, Mo, who is weaving now from left to right in an effort to shield Finn's body from the view of the window, hisses, 'Come on, Finny. This is all I need. Hide that bottle quickly before she comes out again.'

'Hide it! I'm going to fucking drink it,' barks Finn, lowering the bottle to his side. 'And as for her, I'm not worried about her. She's got you right under the cosh,' he says, as if to explain the matter to himself.

Mo shakes his head. Up to now they'd only had harmless encounters but he is angered by Finn's words, yet he would feel disloyal jumping him.

'I've been in nearly every nick in the country,' says Finn, tapping himself on the chest as if this is the greatest achievement anyone can ever hope for.

Mo, considering the consequences if Lucretia should suddenly appear, seeks to appease Finn's dislike of her.

'She's all right really, Finny,' he begins.

'All right!' shouts Finn. 'All right for what? Flashing her arse and having a go at the workers?' He laughs menacingly.

Mo shakes his head slowly. 'It must have been Tampax-talk. She's not usually like that.' The intimate female disclosure sounds sexy coming from Mo, and Finn, who by this time is beginning to get a bit merry, bursts out laughing, deciding that he will continue to wind Mo up. (And her too, if he gets the chance.)

'What you on about, Mo?' he asks, assuming a puzzled frown.

Mo swings his gaze away from Finn's, trying to convince himself that Lucretia's pettiness and irritability were indeed more earthy rather than cerebral. Stemming from below the neck rather than above.

The clusters of branches become piles. The piles become stacks. The heat becomes oppressive, and the lads work steadily on. Several times Finn threatens to quit but Mo always manages to persuade him to stay, reminding him that the longer he works by day the more money he will have to spend by night. Concentrating on hacking through a particularly thick section of the tree, Mo doesn't see Lucretia come out of the house until he hears Finn's loud, cheeky whistle of appreciation, which causes him to jerk upright. Without a word passing between them they both lean heavily on the handles of their axes, staring at Lucretia who is setting up a sunbed a few feet away from them, for the felled tree still dominates the entire garden.

'I have a phone-in client to deal with in an hour,' she says, looking at her watch in a superior way. 'And it's such a beautiful day. A pity to be inside. So I think I'll just relax.' With that she lies down on the lounger and, stretching out her long, sun-starved body, unfurls a copy of *Yoga Weekly*. But before burying her head in its pages she glances severely over at the lads.

If this is intended to set them harder to their task it has the opposite effect as Finn, putting down his axe, lights a butt, leans casually against the tree and speaks. 'Hot, innit?'

She ignores him.

Finn looks at Mo, then they both continue to gaze fixedly at Lucretia who, after a while, looks up at them coldly. The lads grin back stupidly.

'Do you find something about me surprising? Something different? Or is it just that you are both badly in need of therapy?' She says this with all the disapproval of a nun who's just caught a Peeping Tom watching her adjusting her habit.

'No, no,' says Finn straightening up. 'We . . . we—'

'We were wondering . . . Are you interested in yoga?' interrupts Mo quickly, fearing that she might connect Finn's stutter with drink. It is a sensible question and obviously should receive a sensible answer.

'Yes, I am,' she replies. And then, suspiciously, 'Are you?', feeling suddenly irritated that these two labourers who had obviously been ogling her body should suddenly profess interest in the nature of the Absolute.

'Do you know anything about breath control, then?' asks Finn, bubbling with enthusiasm.

Lucretia sits bolt upright, looking at him. 'I'm more interested in birth control,' she replies, before going back to her magazine.

Finn squirms. The man who's been in nearly every nick in the country still hasn't got used to being closely supervised. He mumbles incoherently, clearing his throat and spitting on the ground. If Lucretia thinks she's going to relax she doesn't know yet that she's in the company of one of the city's leading flop-house philosophers.

Finn continues to clear his throat noisily. 'It's a well-known fact of nature that most babies are born male. What's your view on that?' he asks.

Lucretia throws her magazine down and, picking up a

160

pair of shears, continues grandly, 'I'm not prepared to argue hypothetical cases with you, nor disclose my view nor the views of the manual held by our group in higher esteem than all the male ramblings of the Bible and the other so-called holy books put together.'

'Phew,' says Finn. 'I'm glad to hear it.'

'You are?' says Lucretia, surprised.

'Yes. It's some relief to know that you're not totally influenced by the methods of King Herod.'

Lucretia gives him a cheery smile. 'No. We abhor barbarity and intend a more humane solution through the teachings of the Koran.'

'You'd resort to Allah?' exclaims Finn, flabbergasted.

'No. The Caliph of Baghdad – whose methods for preventing the male workforce becoming too amorous with the women of the harem were thorough,' replies Lucretia, snipping the air politely with the garden shears.

'You're talking balls.'

'Exactly!' cries Lucretia primly.

Finn unconsciously puts his hand deep into his pocket, a look of reassurance crossing his face. Lucretia's laugh echoes round the garden as it starts to rain. Relieved, she rises and disappears into the house.

Mo looks at the sky as the rain pours down. Finn chuckles. 'Looks like it's set in for the rest of the day,' he says, shouldering his axe, grabbing the saw and making for the shed. After picking up the shears and his own axe, Mo follows. Finn, not wishing to appear too eager to quit, lights a butt, up-ends an old apple box and sits himself down. Mo, awaiting events, does likewise.

But the rain continues to fall, fast and furious. 'We'd better be going, then,' says Mo finally.

After he's been paid off Finn turns to Mo. 'Don't forget that lift business,' he says with a wink.

'Have some tea,' says Lucretia to Mo after Finn has left. 'Perhaps you could work on the shelving for the remainder of the day?'

As Mo begins sawing a strut, an idea for completing a tricky passage of dialogue in his book is forming in his mind. As he is pondering, Lucretia, noting that his left hand seems in line with the saw, shouts excitedly, 'Oh! Mind your hand! We don't want symmetry before safety.'

Mo moves his hand abruptly. He's completely charmed that for a moment he seems to have become the centre of her attention. 'Thanks for the warning.'

'Well, you might sue me,' she says.

Mo looks pained. 'Perhaps you really would be better off with someone else doing this job for you,' he says sadly.

Lucretia moves close. 'Oh, don't you want to help me?' she coaxes, with an appealing expression.

'I'm not sure,' says Mo slowly. 'I get confused by your moods.'

'By my what?' shrieks Lucretia, her voice raised to a shout. 'How dare you say such a thing? You've become much more outspoken since you first came round here.'

Mo looks intensely at the plan for the shelves. 'I can't help it. I got slung out of hospital over it. They're not too keen on that sort of thing there either.'

'Neither am I. I must have gentle people around me.' A light breeze wafts through the open window. Lucretia gives a few tuneful sneezes.

Mo smiles. 'Italians sing, even when they sneeze.'

'Are we being silly?' says Lucretia, hiding a smile.

Mo laughs. 'Did you get any more screws?' he asks, searching around among the timber.

'Yes. There was no one serving. I couldn't hang around so I took these. God helps those who help themselves,' she says, winking naughtily at Mo.

'Yes. And God help those who get caught helping themselves. Like my mate Nose Job who's just got six months.'

Lucretia blinks. 'Oh, it's a police state,' she says, solemnly. 'Lesbians and gays are persecuted groups.'

'So are dossers.'

'Sorry? Could you please repeat that? Decoded for the benefit of the less informed.'

162

'Homeless people,' says Mo. 'They're persecuted all right. And the biggest section of people in nick are working-class blokes.'

Lucretia laughs derisively. 'Pity they can't claim diplomatic immunity.'

'What?' says Mo, not sure whether she's joking. 'Isn't that just for middle-class people?'

'What are you talking about? Where did you hear about middle-class people claiming immunity?' says Lucretia.

'Well,' says Mo, taking a pencil from behind his ear and marking the bore holes for a strut, 'they're claiming everything else nowadays.'

'Never believe what you see in the papers. They're all right-wing publications. You should read *Borough Boundaries* or *Seconds Out*.'

Mo looks at her sharply. 'What for? I'm not bent or a pseudo lefty.'

'Oh, so you like the girls, do you? Is that it? Tut, tut,' she says, clicking her tongue with irritation.

'Of course I do. What's wrong with that?' asks Mo, with more than a little surprise.

'Not very intellectual, is it? For someone who wishes to be a writer,' she says, with a look of mock concern. Concentrating on levelling a shelf Mo does not bother to answer.

Lucretia has suddenly become exasperated. She is trying unsuccessfully to open a tin of cat food. She looks round at Mo. 'Can you open this for me? The tin opener's broken.' Mo, taking the tin from her, grabs the shelving hammer, smashing it into the top of the can. Lucretia shrieks in horror. 'What are you doing?' She rushes over to him. 'Stop! Your methods might have worked wonders at Waterloo but they're far too advanced for Hampstead.'

'But I've opened it a bit,' says Mo, laughing. 'Let's just force it a bit more now and—'

The phone rings and Lucretia walks over to it, shouting over her shoulder, 'OK. But remember it's not the Gordian knot.' Then, picking up the receiver, she speaks into it. 'Hello? Oh, hello, Sophie. Oh, good. Really? Yes, I've still got my young man here with me.' She looks round teasingly at Mo. 'Oh, by the way, Sophie, Mark Lane and Sarah Stone are only inviting intellectual types to dinner in future. Yes, they say they're fed up with boring people. Of course I saw their last play. Oh, I don't know what to think of it. Hard to put it into words, really. All so *avant-garde*. Perhaps it's too advanced for its time? Sorry? Oh, yes, yes. It would be great to see more women writers of that calibre. She's terrific.' Lucretia lowers her voice. 'Her explanation of the female orgasm is startling. Oh, I agree. One should always try to remain detached during love-making, simply to see which orgasm, if any, one experiences at such times. Sorry? Oh, I see. No. No, it only makes for clammy, sentimental bedroom scenes. Best left alone. Oh, I will, I will. OK, then. Bye!'

Lucretia anchors the phone and goes over to the coat-stand. 'I'll see you tomorrow, Mo,' she says, putting on her coat. 'I've got to run.'

Lucretia is annoyed when Mo arrives for work the next day. Understandably so, perhaps, as he is three hours late. 'So you're here at last!' She rounds on him irritably as she opens the door. 'Another one who can't get out of bed in the mornings.'

Mo wishes now that he'd stayed in bed, especially since he'd had hardly any sleep again during the night.

After closing the door, Lucretia turns, breaking off her scolding abruptly as she looks in open-mouthed wonder to where Mo has sat down, sprawling in the chair, head lolling on to his shoulder. She steps over, peering into his face. 'Are you ill?' she enquires, her voice hovering between vexation and compassion.

'No, no. I'm OK,' says Mo, jerking upright and prising himself out of the chair. 'Sorry I'm late. I never got to sleep until six o'clock this morning.'

'Really,' says Lucretia, staring at him as if this is the most intimate disclosure he could ever have revealed to her about himself. There is certainly an element of danger here, she feels sure. What, she asks herself, was he doing during normal sleeping hours?

'I'm OK now, though,' shrugs Mo, flexing his shoulders and straightening his back to emphasise just how wide awake he is. Lucretia, still scrutinising Mo, is beginning to get worried. Perhaps a professional might indeed be safer in the long run? Hadn't Nadia mentioned something about a chequered past? Some questions, however awkward, must be asked.

'Mo,' says Lucretia slowly, fiddling with the folds of her dress, 'why did you not go to bed well before six o'clock this morning?'

'Oh, I went to bed well before six,' replies Mo miserably, as he runs his eye over the shelves he's constructing. 'In fact, I was in bed well before midnight, but someone in the house had a win on the horses and they all came back drunk. No one got any sleep after that.'

At this Lucretia's expression softens. 'Well, I never,' she says. 'Tell me, do your neighbours often throw such impromptu parties?'

'Quite often,' says Mo, trying to stifle a yawn.

'But what about the landlord? Doesn't he intervene?'

Mo gives her a tired smile. 'The landlord only calls to collect the rent.'

'And how much rent do you pay?'

'Fifty pound a week,' says Mo.

'That's quite a lot for a room in a noisy house,' replies Lucretia, who is becoming quite thoughtful about Mo's accommodation. Like most middle-class types, she has curious ways of steering a conversation.

'The DHSS pays it, not me,' says Mo. 'It's expensive, but you live where you can. I couldn't afford to pay it.'

'And how about you, Mo?' probes Lucretia. 'Do you drink?'

'Not any more,' says Mo, shaking his head solemnly.

With a satisfied look, Lucretia begins to fill the kettle. 'You shall have a cup of tea before you start,' she says, switching it on. Adding in the same breath, 'Why don't you come and live here?' She smiles openly at Mo as she says this. 'It's very quiet, and you would be able to write much better.'

Mo can't believe his ears – in fact, he thinks for a second that she's joking. But Lucretia is far from joking. She can discard her class position when the need arises to pounce on any crumb of advantage afforded to the working class before climbing back smartly to straddle more firmly the horse of class dignity. Bourgeois refinement is all very well – but doctors can be struck off, priests defrocked, kings dethroned. Yes, she thinks still smiling encouragingly at Mo. A man with the full backing of the Social Security behind him. Such a one will always have money to pay the rent . . .

'Well. Now we've sorted you out someone's got to get on with some work,' she says. 'I've got to visit one of my clients and this place is in such a mess. Oh, everything's so hectic.' She looks at Mo thoughtfully. 'Mo, will you do something for me?'

'What is it?'

'Be an angel and finish the washing-up for me before you start on the shelves.' And taking a flowered apron off a hook she thrusts it at him. 'You can put this on.'

Mo jerks back as if from a punch. 'No. I won't need it,' he says.

'Of course you will,' she chides. 'It'll keep you clean.'

Reluctantly, Mo takes it from her outstretched hand. And with that she's gone.

Mo stands there dressed in the apron. A chess player whose last move has somehow robbed him of the initiative. Angrily he shoves his hands into the sink and begins to scrub the crockery. He suddenly becomes aware that he is being watched by Max, who at some point must have come into the room.

'It's a big subject. But that's what makes the world go round,' says Max, making an expansive gesture with his hands. 'Love. Or is it sex? Never quite sure about that one. Still, everybody craves intense experience sometime. Don't you agree?'

Mo's eyes steady on him. 'I don't know about that.'

Max laughs. 'I must admit some women's methods for achieving their own ends are not quite as white as the driven snow. Some men say they'd rather have a nice clean boy any day. Far less complicated.' He cocks his eye at Mo. 'Even gardeners need to make their own luck sometimes.'

'Sod that lark,' says Mo, with some annoyance. 'I keep away from all that.'

Max grins. 'Oh, come, come. You'll need to be a bit more broad-minded if you intend to embark – never mind succeed – on a literary career. The publishing world's notorious for it.'

'I hope it's not compulsory,' says Mo offhandedly.

'Beautiful women for bed? It's all a fantasy. The Virgin Mary only appeared once and that was in France. Looks like you've missed her this time round, Mo.'

'Oh, well. I'll have to make do with farting, burping and sneezing until she comes again.'

Max stares at Mo, slightly bemused by his quick-witted abruptness. 'You don't think much of me, do you?' he asks, suddenly. 'But you'd better watch out.' His tone becomes sinister.

'What you on about?' asks Mo.

'That's how I started, sonny,' he replies, indicating Mo's apron. 'Tough I used to be. Up at dawn. A few press-ups on the sideboard. A trot round the block before the cornflakes. A bit of Kung Fu. Cold showers if I felt too randy. That sort of thing.'

'Get to the point,' says Mo with a casualness he did not feel. 'I'm busy.'

'Oh. I was busy too in those days,' confides Max. 'Not a moment to spare. Oh, yes. I even joined night classes.'

Mo looks at him.

'New experience. The women tasty yet educated. High heels replaced by high IQs. Then I met Lucretia. Like a spiritual awakening it was. Bliss. Eventually she got me into that apron.' He points at Mo. 'I didn't like it. Hated it, really. But a flash of leg here, a bit of cleavage there. Promise of better things to come. You know how it is.'

'You mean you never got anywhere?'

'Oh, yes. She was as good as her word. Better in fact.' Max pushes his hand through his hair. 'She can be all woman when she wants. Well, to cut it short, she's five months gone. I was over the moon. The birds sang sweeter over Highgate Wood. If a vagrant begged me for 10p he got a pound . . . A smile for the rent man. A nod to the—'

'Yeah. OK. Happy days.' Mo is impatient for the punch-line.

'Indeed they were. Then one evening I came home early from the parentcraft class. She'd gone. Looked everywhere I did. At last I found her. I was shocked when I saw her. Stomach flat as a board. Face white.' Max shakes his head. 'Not the same girl at all. Oh, no.'

The only sound in the room is the drip of a faulty tap.

'What happened?' asks Mo quietly. 'Miscarriage?'

Max shrugs. 'Whatever it was it seems to have given her more experience in her job.' He looks cunningly at Mo, still standing by the sink, his face confused, mind elsewhere.

'Happy days,' chirps Max hollowly as he leaves the room.

Of course there are many reasons for becoming bewildered, but falling in love causes the most bewilderment of all, subjecting us to many an hour of refined torture. Although people are repeatedly exposed to this most basic of human flaws they continually fail to grasp its lesson.

The acoustics are all wrong again. The amplified sound is blaring. The trains will be late because of either fire, signal failure, collision, or perhaps a body on the line. The announcer's indecipherable squawk never makes the reason clear. The station is dotted with shabby figures, who every now and then stop their aimless amblings to form into downcast little groups. Bellies churning, tobacco burning throats and eyes, waiting for the soup run or to bum the cost of a Sally bed. Sticks Moloney, old but vibrant, avoids flop-houses and steers clear of hand-out grub whenever possible . . . no vitamins in it nowadays anyways. Just enough artificial protein to keep them moving. The litter-bins overspill their dark contents on to the tiled concourse floor. Sidling up he plunges his hand into the nearest one, dragging from it a half-eaten peanut butter sandwich. What a find! The ultimate in protein. He stuffs it into his mouth, nearly severing two fingers in the process. As he wolfs it down a strange feeling of light-headedness comes over him . . . With five more bins to go he hopes he hasn't peaked too soon.

Moloney continues to graze, dipping his hand among each bin's assorted delights. A few nuts here, a crushed Big Mac leftover there. He isn't eating anywhere else any more. After exchanging a few pleasantries with an up-the-country dosser who says he is looking for work, Moloney (well-fed and rested now) decides to do some himself. The mere fact of survival imposes crime. Sidestepping to avoid the crush of passengers in a hurry he begins to indulge in an impersonal commercial transaction with the rest.

'Is that you, Ali?' The voice calls out as the sarge sits having a smoke on the sly in the builder's temporary toilet. Ali. The name floats round the urinal setting off nervous vibes, conjuring up all sorts of ancient taboos. Not a name like Michael or John, Bill or Rupert, even – a name that some mother has put a bit of Christian thought into, muses the sarge, irritable at being disturbed. After a few more puffs he spits the butt out of his mouth and screws his heel on it. Pulling the chain, he notices its strengthless flush, the cistern corroded red-rotten with rust arousing security-conscious disgust. Time to get back on the rounds. A little walking never hurt anyone, and he needs to see how that new rookie, PC Bates, is getting on.

The sergeant stands stock still when he spots it, leaving his newest recruit to carry on walking a further step or two before he notices it too. Emblazoned six feet high and three feet wide across the wall of the tunnel leading to the entrance of the eastern subway is a voluptuous blonde nymph, semi-draped in some sort of fibreglass armour, her midriff flat and bare. Her long, slim legs, with their muscles taut and rippling, are firmly gripped around a winged rocket. A wise if somewhat arrogant smile plays on her lips, presumably showing contempt for those who still travel by train.

'Who put that there?' roars the sarge. 'Fucking graffiti artists. What kind of minds have they got?' He shakes his head. 'I ask you – they've got to be twisted to do something like that.'

PC Bates lets his gaze rove slowly over it before replying, his look conveying a technical interest in perspective, colour, form and detail. 'Oh, I don't know. A little futuristic, perhaps, but quite a worthy subject matter, really, I would have thought,' he finally answers.

The sergeant turns slowly to face him. 'Constable,' he begins, emphasising each word with a stab of his finger on the new recruit's chest, 'this is a hint you can take as advice. It's perverted – that's what it is.' He pulls at his chinstrap. 'Where's it all start and where's it all going to end?' he mumbles to himself dejectedly.

'Well,' replies the constable blithely, 'I suppose it was all started by the upper classes in the Dark Ages – yes, about then, I should think.'

'What are you on about, lad? It wasn't even there this time last week.'

'No, I mean the concept, sarge. The ruling classes used to proclaim themselves and map out their own patch with it – coats of arms, sort of medieval codes. Yes, it was all very complicated and colourful, governed by strict sets of rules, many of which are in force even to this day.' The constable begins to look sheepish. 'Got an A in art at school,' he adds quietly.

It isn't clear from his expression whether the sergeant is interested or just plain puzzled by his constable's remarks, and because he remains silent the constable decides to continue. 'Yes, very strict rules. Same as the ones which govern latter-day heraldry or graffiti art now. They'd never use a stencil, copy another's work or use the same design twice. Sometimes they spend a whole year working on a piece.'

'They'll get a lot more than a year if I get my hands on them,' explodes the sergeant. He then adopts a more reasoned tone, suited to their debate. 'It creates a threatening environment, gives passengers a feeling of insecurity.'

'Yes, but there's different schools of thought on that, sarge. All spray-can art tries to avoid falling into the trap of commanding attention through overt sentimentality.'

The sergeant is getting a little worried by his underling's use of words and hopes he hasn't been lumbered with a wrong 'un. Perhaps he's just a bit too good-looking, in a delicate sort of way.

'Constable, it's still vandalism whatever way you look at it.'

172

'Yes, from our point of view that's true. Even so, I'm convinced that just as Mozart could – within the restrictions of a few notes – create sounds of incomparable beauty, a talented kid like Narcissus One can produce exquisite little cameos of twentieth-century art.'

The only thing the sergeant is convinced about now is that he's been landed with a fairy. He needs a reassuring cup of tea.

'Let's put that café under surveillance before we take a ride on the Central Line.'

As they go up the escalator, the sarge tentatively reopens the conversation. 'Who's this Narcissus One when he's at home, then? Tell me what you know about him, he seems a bit of a lad.'

As they proceed, the constable explains how Narcissus got his name. The 'One' says it all, really. There is no other graffiti artist like him. He is the absolute best, called Narcissus because of his exclusive use of a brightly coloured reflecting paint.

After they've ordered their food, they find an empty table near the window where the sarge can keep an eye on the station hall.

'So, you got an A for art, constable,' says the sarge, taking a bite of his cheese roll and washing it down with a slug of tea.

'Yes, at school, then a year at college before joining the Force.' He looks thoughtfully into the sugar bowl. 'Wanted to make a career out of it but there's no money in art while you're learning.' He begins twisting the bowl, altering its shadow on the table.

'I suppose that's one reason for kids turning to graffiti.' He throws an apologetic smile at the sergeant, who nods for him to continue. 'That's where they get most of their experience. See, no graphic art firm worth its salt is going to employ them until they've done at least a year's apprenticeship on the streets or down the tube.'

'Is that so?' muses the sarge. 'And where, I wonder, do they get the money for the paint?'

'Oh, it's not too dear, sarge. The younger kids use cheap

car-spray cans. From the lowest to the highest, we all try to express what we feel the best way we can. Can't all do it in the Chapel.'

'What?'

'Sorry, I was thinking of Michelangelo, sarge,' says the rookie. In answer to the sergeant's puzzled look, he adds, 'He painted pictures on the ceiling of the Sistine Chapel.'

'God Almighty,' whispers the sergeant. 'Graffiti on the roof of a church.'

'He was commissioned, sarge.'

'Commissioned!' roars the sarge. 'That's no excuse – I'd have him committed.'

'Well, maybe, but the most important aspect is that they feel they are putting a mark, their name or a tag on something. They will go to any lengths to do this; any clear space or stretch of wall will do to emboss their stuff. As they get more skilful they begin using a better medium – a non-drip, non-slip paint known as Dip 4. Sometimes at night when the system's turned off, especially at weekends, a gang will go out to the depot and start bossing their tag. A hit is scored when a carriage completely covered with murals is taken out of commission.'

The sarge drains his cup, banging it down on the table. He gets up. 'It's beyond belief what's happening nowadays. Come on, let's get over to the central zone before the rush hour starts.' He gives the rookie an almost tender smile. 'You done well to join the Force, lad,' he says, patting the young copper's shoulder affectionately. 'I dread to think what would have become of you if you'd stayed on at that art college.'

Dawn is just breaking over the depot as Narcissus One puts the final touches to his mural, strobing his can gently to create illusions of light.

In another corner of the carriage, Bat-moth sits watching the master work. In spite of certain eccentricities that one exhibits at the age of twelve and a half, he is extremely shrewd and always aware that he can grasp in minutes what takes other kids years. Now he considers how Narcissus holds his can to avoid spill as he layers the paint to create savage realism. Yes, understanding is coming slowly but surely to Bat.

The younger kids are spread around the carriage spraying at random, daubing around, bossing their tag, when a shout from outside makes them all jump.

'Quick – it's the law!' whispers Bat.

Dropping their cans, they spring from the carriage, running the few yards to the base of an embankment topped by a low, steel-meshed fence. Breathlessly they clamber up the embankment. Stopping by the fence to look back at their pursuers, relief shows on every face as they see the lone copper standing between the carriages. Fear dwindling, they are confident now that they can jump the fence with ease before the sergeant can reach the bottom of the embankment. The youngsters begin indulging in a bit of high jinks – cheering, laughing and jitter-bugging about, giving the old copper, who hasn't even started across the rails yet, the V sign. The sergeant gives no indication of his mood as he watches this show of youthful high spirit. After a while, his neutral attitude becomes apparent even to the excited youngsters. Without an opposing player, where is the game? One after another, they stop their teasing and turn to mount the fence. That's when the sergeant uncorks his surprise.

Springing up from where they've been hiding behind piles

of stacked sleepers, a dozen or so of his men make a rush towards the fence.

Like fledgelings before the beaters, the kids panic, scrambling pell-mell back down the scrub-soiled embankment. Even in their haste they realise the trap, angling their run so they'll land at the bottom of a clear stretch of track hoping to avoid being driven into the sergeant's long arms.

With the constables marking them from the top and the sergeant bringing up the rear, the kids tear along the track, running zig-zag between the rails. Young and fit, they are easily putting distance between themselves and their pursuers.

Narcissus One is so far in the lead that he decides to treat himself to a backward glance – a swift glance. But the momentary loss of concentration causes him to miss his footing. Stumbling against a rail, he falls.

The other kids freeze as the current in the form of a brilliant blue flash hits him full blast. Twisting crazily, his body bucks twice then lies still, stretched across the rails, hair sticking straight out from his head like porcupine quills.

The kids stand like figures in a frieze, hardly daring to breathe as the police come up behind them.

'Well, so much for art,' says the sergeant, looking down at the lifeless body.

'Jesus!' exclaims a clearly freaked PC Bates. 'What's the power doing on?'

The sergeant looks at him sharply. 'New games, new rules, lad. Best security you can get at any price. Especially if you crank the juice up an amp or two at night.'

Dead painters don't spray, trains arrive late and depart on time or vice versa *ad infinitum*. Some things change, others stay the same. (Soon after the tragedy, PC Bates left the Force.)

Eaten inside by the memory of their dead friend and the tiger of desire – even in the face of the sergeant's massive security precautions – every graffiti gang member swears that they will boss their tag on every train every day in honour of their dead friend Narcissus One.

But as the days turn into weeks and the weeks into months the trains remain unmarked. 'And that's the way I like it,' the sergeant is often heard to say in the Briefing Room, staring down fiercely at his squad of short-cropped rookies' heads.

The Piccadilly Line train is just beginning to close its doors as the two coppers enter the platform.

'God in heaven – what the bloody hell is that?' roars the sergeant, staring as if transfixed at a dramatic but macabre painting on the tube's door depicting, amid wild and jagged forked tongues of lightning, the nude upper halves of a young man and woman's bodies, their lower extremities those of lion and tigress.

The sarge stares mouth open as the doors' complete closure draws – with serene indifference – the figures into a tight, erotic embrace.

He continues to gaze open-mouthed while the train, lurching as it pulls away, gives the painted flesh an impression of movement.

'It's diabolical – that's what it is,' he keeps repeating as he makes his way back to the Charge Room to compile his report.

'Everything OK, sarge?' asks the duty copper pleasantly enough.

The sarge looks hard at him before replying peevishly, 'You into power dressing or something, Constable Pike?' He motions with his notebook at the duty copper's jacket which he's draped casually over his back, shoulders sticking up in the air, sleeves hanging limply down.

'Sorry, sarge,' says PC Pike, slipping his hands into the sleeves and buttoning the jacket up.

'Good. Now, if you're ready, I want you to type up a report for the Divisional Inspector.'

When PC Pike is seated behind the typewriter the sergeant begins. 'A violation has occurred by a person or persons as yet unknown to an item of London Regional

Transport property, namely rolling stock, to wit a train, specifically one pair of metal carriage doors . . .'

And so begins the sergeant's blue period and the painters' multi-coloured one. Each week brings forth a new mural, larger and more daring than the rest. Although hardly up to the artistic level of Narcissus One, the paintings are, none the less, most vivid and talented sprays full of symbolism. Definitely in the School of Narcissus and it isn't long before everybody begins to call the new lowlife maestro Narcissus Two.

The sergeant has the outlying depots under constant surveillance – power on full blast night and day. But the murals continue to appear on the side of the carriages and then the unbelievable happens – they begin appearing on the offside.

'It's impossible!' cries the sergeant when it's reported to him. Impossible or not, it is so, as he finds to his horror when he goes to investigate. No matter how much he puzzles over it he cannot work it out.

Mole has been living down the tube too long. Anyone can see that. You can tell by the way he walks and moves, sloth-like to slow the energy seeping from his jaded pores. Never takes two steps where one will do – same with all his actions.

Mole always seems to appear from nowhere, sidling up beside a passenger to beg; his face long and sad, crinkled and yellow from the sunless heat. They've discharged Mole from the mental hospital. The theory is that he'll recover faster on the streets but Mole has a lot to recover from.

Eventually he gets a job in advertising, earning enough for a few pints and a meal trundling around the West End with a sandwich board slung across his bony back warning of the sins of the flesh activated by the lust-producing proteins latent in meat. Mole has to resign after he's got the dosser's equivalent of executive stress – sandwich-board fatigue.

Mole is continually hungry no matter how many litter bins he sifts through. His appetite is never appeased. He tried the Hare Krishna mob once or twice – probably influenced by his former employment's cautionary logo – but the acolytes seemed to think that it's stretching Krishna's teachings (all-embracing as they may be) a little too far to include the likes of Mole in their temple for a free vegan lunch.

It's hard to believe there isn't a scrap, not a crumb in any of the bins. Mole is ravenous – he'll have to go back over to the Jubilee Line where he thinks, though his memory isn't too sharp (his eyesight is worse), that he missed a bin earlier on. He wanders away to get a bite before he gets a touch of the staggers. It's Tuesday and the cleaners have been thorough, attentive to their tasks, mindful of their superior's warnings.

Mole sits up against the platform's tiled wall wagging his head from side to side having a dry cry as a train pulls to a stop in front of him. From his position on the floor his eyes are level, on account of the raised stretch of track, with the train's undercarriage and wheels. Wheels that can crush the life from a man like the ice-cream cone squelched flat, forming a sticky mess on one of the rims.

What is he doing, where is he going and who cares, anyway? People think more of their dogs. Mole has never thought such thoughts before and dares to now only because he is demented with hunger. Looking utterly dejected, he begins to crawl forward (drawn, as the sea is said to draw) towards the tracks. Reaching out his hands, he is just about to scrape up the bits of soiled wafer that jut from the squashed ice cream when he sees a face staring back at him between the wheels.

Mole gives no sign of fear or shock until the train has pulled away. Then, not seeing what he expected to see, his eyes widen, like a child's. No matter how hard he looks there's no one there. He glances swiftly after the train – nothing, no one around anywhere, the opposite platform completely empty. Forlorn but resilient, Mole struggles to his feet muttering to himself. He is about to shamble off when the bright red shiny canister nestling between the rails catches his eye.

Mole seldom drinks, tending to eat instead. It has got to be a habit though, and hunger pangs force him to a reluctant decision. He will have to go aloft. After all, a little change of air might do him good. He shuffles towards the exit escalator. A peeling wanted poster takes his eye. 'Wanted for Murder' the caption says. Unable to read, the words mean nothing to Mole. What attracts him are the eyes in the youthful face: hunted and tense they stare out. When Mole was carrying the sandwich board around he was told it said something about food. Perhaps the youth in the poster had been picked, because he looks so hungry, to advertise a new food hand-out. In his frustration Mole begins to trace his finger over the words hoping this may somehow impart a clue.

A train pulls to a stop with a squeal of brakes. Mole moves closer to the poster to avoid crowd surge. As the crowds veer round him he hitches up his trousers. Several conversations float by. He thinks of asking someone what the poster says. He's found that the posher the voice the better its owner can read — at least their paper was usually larger.

Amid the jumble of sounds Mole does not hear the plain-clothes man slink up behind him until he feels a pair of hands, one grasping his coat collar, the other his hair. 'What you up to, you daft bastard?' whispers the copper, at the same time bashing Mole's face into the poster on the wall.

A terrible stench fills the Charge Room, clogging all the coppers' nostrils, when the plain-clothes man pushes Mole through its doors. 'What's he been up to?' asks the duty copper, holding his hand to his nose. 'Wait, let me guess. Been bin-bugging, begging, no? Failing to adjust his attire before travel, public nuisance.'

Mole puts his fingers up to his bruised face indicating that it was the tec's doing. 'I bet,' quips the duty copper's flash colleague, 'it's statutory rape.'

'Yeah,' smirks the other, 'she was standing still at the time.'

'Put up a good fight though by the looks of his face.'

'He's being done for damaging transport property,' says the detective. 'Caught him defacing a Serious Crime poster.' He jerks his thumb in Mole's direction. 'Can you handle it, Pikey?'

'OK, turn out your pockets,' says the duty copper with a world-weary sigh.

Mole begins to comply as Pike's colleague writes in the Prisoners' Property Book. 'One empty matchbox, one piece of string, frayed, a broken watchstrap, one . . . wait a minute, what exactly is that?' says the cop after Mole puts a small figurine on the desk. 'Here, Tom, is that a leprechaun, a pixie, an elf or what?'

'Search me,' says Tom, scratching at his closely shorn scalp. ''Tain't a wizard, is it?'

'Or . . . here, maybe it's a genie, that's what it is.'

'It's Shiva,' says Mole quietly. The two coppers look at him. 'A lucky Eastern god.'

'OK, one East End god.'

'Now, let's get on with the other pocket.'

'One plastic comb skeleton, no teeth. One . . . well, what have we got here?' says PC Pike as Mole produces a red spray-paint can. Whistling soundlessly he picks up the phone and speaks into it. 'George, yeah, is the old man there? Tell him he's wanted in the Charge Room.'

'What's that filthy stink doing in my office?' shouts the sergeant choosing not to acknowledge Mole standing at the desk. Mole wisely does not reply.

'Look what we found in his pocket, sarge,' says PC Pike holding out the spray can. The sergeant takes it from him and, removing the cap with a flourish, presses the plunger down releasing a spume of bright red paint that goes all over the front of Mole's ragged coat. Mole recoils more from the aggressive intent in the action rather than the ruination of his only clothing.

The sergeant, holding the can's nozzle carelessly near Mole's eyes, stares unemotionally into his face. 'You'd have done yourself and everybody else concerned a big favour if you'd used it like that. To keep the stink down instead of defacing our trains with that dirty scribbling.'

'I've not done anything to the trains,' mumbles Mole.

'Did he say something?' asks the sarge looking over at PC Pike.

Pike is right on cue. 'I think he said he would like to sign a confession.' Mole's head jerks up at him. 'After he's had a fag, of course, and one of our nice meals.'

'He would, would he?' says the sarge to PC Pike, both apparently heedless of Mole's quiet but firm denials. 'Well, then,' says the sarge pulling out a packet of fags and offering them to Mole. 'Go on, help yourself.' Mole, unable to resist the nagging desire, automatically shoots out a hand plucking a fag from the packet. He puts it between his lips waiting expectantly for a light. Again, the sarge decides not to acknowledge Mole, and walks over to the constable. 'Make a phone call to the canteen, will you, Pikey?' And, of course, the constable picks up the phone as he is told. After more chat than seems strictly necessary, he has to check with the sergeant what Mole would like to order. The sarge snatches the telephone out of his hand and shouts into the mouthpiece. 'Never mind the duck with orange sauce, we got a hungry chummie up here helping with inquiries and he wants something substantial, as in sustaining. Got it? Let's have something pronto.' He puts the phone down, turning with a smile. 'Soon be here. When did you last eat, old son?'

While they wait for Mole's dinner, the questioning continues. But there seems to be some mix-up in communications with the canteen. The staff have gone home early, so Mole's order never comes.

The sarge says he will send the constable across to the café outside for something, but since he isn't familiar with Mole's culinary likes and dislikes he has to ask. Mole explains that what he really likes, what sets his tastebuds on fire, is good old-fashioned soup and that if they didn't feel too upset about it he would go down to the hand-out right that minute and get his own. But this turns out to be a very serious breach of etiquette on his part, and they throw him into a cell for the night without any supper.

'I'm a fair man,' says the sergeant when they begin the next morning. 'I'm also prepared to let bygones be bygones, even though you have messed us all about and wasted all our valuable time.' He puts his hand up as Mole tries to speak. 'Wait, let's not get off to a bad start again. This is a new day. We don't want to spoil it by beginning it with falsehoods, do we?' He pushes his face up to Mole, who has mumbled something under his breath. 'What's that?'

'No,' says Mole wiping at his watery eyes.

'Good, so before we speak let's be very careful what we're going to say, shall we, because we now have a reliable eye-witness.' Mole's head shoots up. He looks puzzled. 'A Welsh snuff grinder,' continues the sergeant, 'who just happened to be up in London visiting his optician on the day the offences were committed.'

Mole begins to bite his lip and find his fingers very interesting. 'So now I'm going to ask you why you sprayed all our nice clean trains with paint and the constable here who you met yesterday will write it all down neat and tidy in his best handwriting. Then I'll get you to sign or make your mark against it.'

'Why?' asks Mole suddenly.

'Why?' repeats the sergeant, obviously flabbergasted by the question and missing Mole's accusing tone. '*Why?* So as we don't all forget it when we go into court tomorrow.' Mole looks dejected. 'We're all in this together, you know. You, me and Constable Pike and all the witnesses.'

'All one big family, as it were,' PC Pike adds, helpfully.

Seen in haste between a train's wheels, Mole's face has worried Narcissus Two badly. Thinking they are on to him he begins to see ghosts. Ghosts in blue shirts and dark uniforms hiding behind every train wheel. After that his brushes begin turning hard in their paint jars and the sprays lie still in their cans.

Then his dear old mum, a nice practical woman who

doesn't believe in ghosts, gets fed up with him lolling around the house all day, under her feet when she's trying to do the washing-up. What, she asks, would have happened if Mozart had seen a mouse on top of his piano and Schubert had imagined that spots on his chin were caused by too much violin instead of women and gin.

'Now, I know you might find this hard to believe,' the sergeant always begins to whoever he happens to be with on patrol when he spots a new mural on a train door, 'there's a certain place, out foreign it is, where a stick planted in the ground casts no shadow at noon.' This always brings forth a barrage of questions with which to pass the graffiti silently by.

Graffiti, murals, spray-can art, tagging, bossing, painting, whatever the name, to the rest of the coppers they seem in the light, artificial as it is, a minor problem. Nothing more, nothing less. Only noticed when they first appear, then forgotten. But to the sergeant they are a personal affront, a real threat, never far from his mind.

He had become obsessed with capturing Narcissus Two.

Narcissus Two looks quickly around the platform. No one about, he clambers down between the tracks, dropping into the 'suicide pit' – the inspection trench under the rails. Just as he disappears, a smartly dressed young air hostess arrives on the platform. Her hair is smoothed into a French pleat, topped by her hat at a fetchingly jaunty angle. She is followed by an old dosser who, plonking himself on a seat by a bin, reaches in for yesterday's newspapers. He then sits, shoulders hunched, reading while he thinks longingly about the fag butts that used to pile up in the chipped and rust speckled sand buckets.

When the platform becomes sufficiently full a train, groaning with metal fatigue, lumbers to a stop. As the passengers begin boarding one side, Narcissus Two pushes himself out the other side between the rails. His intuition sharpened by experience and greatly assisted by hearing, he judges the boarding party to be large, something that always affects the size and quality of his pieces. He is spot on: the crowd is massive. The old dosser is the first to fall in the crush. The young woman panics, trying to turn away from the train. She is pushed backwards by the surge and trampled underfoot with the dosser on the floor, and regained her feet with difficulty.

The minutes tick slowly by. Narcissus Two works on steadily. He might, he thinks, get time to add the angel's wings to the horsewoman's back. His pieces are always so much better when he doesn't have to rush.

Amid the constant buzz punctuated now and then by grunts and groans, the crowd fight frantically in the dry heat to climb aboard. The air hostess, obviously trained in such strategy, struggles gamely, but tube crowds differ from their air-borne counterparts and, falling foul of the muddle in the middle, she is forced by the swirling vortex of human flesh to give ground once more. Her cheeky little hat, perched on the side of her head, defies the mêlée to the last as she goes down.

The doors make a few half-hearted attempts to close before finally cutting through the band of thrashing flesh. Narcissus Two has anticipated well, his finely honed hearing warning him to duck back into the pit at the doors' first laboured hiss. His clothing will be ruined though — his pullover has been snagged on an undercarriage lip.

As the train pulls slowly away, the air hostess, her expensive clothing creased and stained, struggling furiously to gain her feet, pushes down with her arm on the old dosser's head in an attempt to retrieve her hat. In his confusion he grabs for support at the first thing that comes his way. As the last carriage clears the station the air hostess screams hysterically at the dosser on the floor with his fingers curled round her leg.

The dosser's nerves are totally shattered. By the time he's gained his feet, even when he's moved half-way down the platform from the woman, he can't understand why she keeps up her piercing shrieks until, looking down on to the tracks, he sees the human chunks of shredded bloody meat.

The sergeant takes no notice, for once, of the woman at the foot of the escalator with a basket of white

185

heather offering to bring you luck at a price as he rushes to the cordoned-off District Line platform. He reaches the platform to find it full of the usual faces after an accident has occurred. The Fire Brigade, the ambulance services, his own men, the British Transport Commission. Funny, he always thought after such calamities, how one insignificant person can do what they could never do in life – control the combined élite of so many different forces.

As the sergeant gazes down at the bits of mutilated body strewn along the track, PC Pike comes up beside him. 'Looks like he's been through a meat grinder, sarge,' he says. 'Gonna have a hell of a job identifying that lot. Nobody's going to know who he was.' The sergeant shifts uncomfortably. He already knows who it is. Even in death he can't mistake the open sensitive eyes of PC Bates.

The ringing sound, gentle but insistent, forces Mo, curled like a dog at the bottom of the open booth, awake. Opening his eyes, he stares out in hung-over confusion at crowds of people queuing alongside platform three. Mo continues to relieve the boredom of their wait, when, finally detecting the source of the sound, he lunges too fast to his feet, head colliding with the underside of a telephone directory holder. Pain stabs all the way to his stomach as he wrenches the phone off the hook.

'Hello. Who's speaking?' asks a strong, well-modulated male voice.

'What? Who's that?'

'Hello. Who's speaking?'

'Eddie Murphy!' slurs Mo.

'Hi, Eddie, Can you tell us where you're speaking from?'

'Euston Station.'

'Can you tell us what's happening down there at the moment, Eddie?'

Mo's eyes flick over to the well-behaved queue of passengers, some of whom, sensing a floor show, have flopped down on their luggage to await events. Mo, knowing they can hear him, lowers the phone, letting his smile travel slowly the length of the queue. 'Well. There's a lot of people about.'

'So what's happening, then?'

'What?' says Mo, struggling to focus on the question.

'You said people . . . presumably passengers looking for trains?'

Mo staggers against the side of the booth. All he wants is to get back to sleep. 'No, looking for their luggage,' he laughs tipsily.

'What's happening to the luggage?' cajoles the voice.

'The Transport Police. They lift it under the smokescreen

187

of security.' Mo, warming to the cheekiness of his rhetoric, continues, 'And once they get it inside the police station, rifle it. "And that's the way it was found, sir", distraught passengers are told when they come to collect.'

'You're joking, of course,' replies the shocked voice.

The phone slips from Mo's grasp. Fumbling clumsily he scoops it up. 'Of course I'm not joking. Nobody round here's so naïve.' Mo raises his voice when he says this and many of the crowd give humorous if slightly apprehensive looks towards their own luggage.

'Have you been drinking a lot today?' quizzes the voice.

'What's it to you? Who are you, anyway?' gabbles Mo, twisting further into the booth.

There is a long silence. Mo becomes suddenly aware of the familiar night-time sounds of the station. Nocturnal moochers sifting the litter-bins, derelicts ambling, a brace of walking travellers, spasmodic shouts of porters as they bustle along, the heavy clangs of coupling chains and last-minute bolt tightening as trains get under way. The voice, businesslike now, breaks over the sounds. 'Do you realise you're on Capital Radio random calls and you've just made a wally of yourself in front of three and a half million people?'

'So what?' says Mo. 'They must be fucking daft to listen.'

'Well, thank you for entertaining us . . . Give us your address and we'll send you a T-shirt.'

'No, thanks. Got an overcoat instead?' asks Mo, knees buckling as he reaches up to anchor the phone. He crumples to a heap, falling asleep on the floor. This brings uneasy laughter from the now-moving queue, as the telephone, Sword of Damocles, dangles above his head.

It is two days before Mo sobers up enough to realise he's even been drunk. He is lying on the floor in his own room – and that's quite an achievement when you've been prowling around for the best part of a week, looking for a kind face, smashed out of your skull. Without much recollection of how he got home, Mo stays where he is, staring at the whiteness of the ceiling, becoming conscious of an unfamiliar weight on his right arm. Slowly, the memory of it all comes dribbling back.

It was a bad mistake to go near the station, but the pressure he'd felt at being out of his element, drifting between two worlds, suddenly overwhelmed him. To escape, to relax, he'd broken out; only feeling safe enough to do so among his former park mates. They'd certainly been happy to see him, feeling pleased that one of their own had written a book. So pleased, in fact, that when the sergeant came by on his rounds they couldn't contain themselves, making no secret of how Mo had immortalised him in print. Of course they had exaggerated blatantly, but was it just possible that between the white lies, the half-truths and the downright whoppers there might still exist a grain of truth? The sergeant began to dwell on it. Had Mo exposed him and his Dirty Tricks brigade? The more he pondered the more his mind became inflamed. After that, Mo's card was well and truly marked. It had only been a matter of time before the sergeant had caught up with him. He'd arrested Mo on sight with a holding charge of drunk and disorderly, releasing him five hours later without charge but with a fractured arm sustained, it was easily explained, while 'resisting arrest'.

Mo looks down at the plaster cast imprisoning his arm, then back at his surroundings. There isn't much in the room and what there is, is in a mess. But, and Mo is comforted by this, nothing is smashed. Less explaining to do. He clambers up awkwardly, closing the window. Suddenly cold, he gets himself a cup of water from the tap, fighting down the urge to go out for another drink.

A few weeks back he was a writer looking for what every writer's looking for: a publisher. Only now he doesn't even have a manuscript. Lucretia has misplaced it. She'd lowered her eyes, putting her hand lightly on his arm to appear considerate when she told him. But when you haven't got something in your hand and after a while it fails to turn up, the word in the mouth may be 'misplaced', but the word in the mind is 'lost'.

'Lost. Lost. Lost,' mumbles Mo, angrily. Grief, rage, shock slowly overwhelm him at the returning memory as his eyes roam round the room. They light on a half-bottle of wine under a chair, which he has overlooked in his hung-over condition. The happiest, or worst, of all discoveries to an alcoholic. With much anxiety Mo picks up the bottle. Slowly, cackhandedly, he twists out the cork, emptying the bottle's contents down the sink.

Now that he's reached the decision, there is no anxiety at all. The best intentions in the world cannot be accomplished by a weak body and mind. After throwing some water on his face, combing his hair and tidying himself up as best as he can, Mo makes his way, as swiftly as his drowsy fumblings will allow, to the top of the stairs. Quickly averting his face at the sight of Lucretia's open living-room door when he reaches the bottom, he crosses the hall silently and, opening the front door, slips out to buy some painkillers.

On his return he isn't so lucky in dodging the sentries. As he closes the door Lucretia's voice rings out. 'Oh, you're there, are you? Mo, can I see you for a moment?'

She looks up from the vegetables she is preparing as he enters the room. 'We were beginning to wonder what had become of you,' she says, studiously ignoring the fact that his arm is in plaster.

'I had an accident. Been in hospital,' lies Mo. 'Bit mucked up at the moment,' he adds, pushing the arm out in front of him.

'So it seems,' she says, frostily. 'How very inconvenient.' And, an incapacitated horse being unavailable for the plough, she goes back to shelling her peas.

Like a family retainer, he has curbed himself up to now, been passive, peaceful, sober and polite, in his relatively short, temperate life. Better to admit once and for all that a lot of the blame is his own. Becoming enamoured of middle-class women, cultured coquettes, with their social-equality bullshit is, he decides, tantamount to colluding with them.

190

It takes many weeks for Mo's arm to heal and during that time an uneasy truce descends between himself and Lucretia. Mo's eagerness to please starts to wane. He can still talk, but not in the spontaneous way he has been used to. Trapped by the heart to members of a class ruled by the head. Now he is paying the price for overlooking that by adopting their strategy in defending himself with words he is in a minority of one. Being entrenched in his room over his wound for so long has brought other realisations too, but he senses he still has a long way to go.

Chess, yoga, boxing, body-building, photography, girlie magazines, weightlifting . . . A weight lifts from his mind as he vies for position among amateur and advanced hobbyists, to look at and read, at varying speeds, this endless array of colourful magazines. Taking a pen from his pocket, Mo copies addresses from some. Voyeurism, it seems, is built into the human psyche, from the man peering through the keyhole at the girl shedding her clothes, to the naturalist peeping through his telescope at the snake shedding its skin. Another wants to see what will win the three-thirty next day, and yet another wants a peep at the stars.

During the next fortnight five large parcels arrive by special delivery for Mo. After he's struggled up the stairs with the last one, Mo makes himself a cup of tea, seeming thoughtful for the rest of the afternoon. Philippa is a little surprised to find him sitting on the front steps when she comes home from school. Her adolescent curiosity aroused, she listens intently as Mo, with his hand round her shoulders, whispers in her ear.

'I'm not sure I could do that,' says Philippa quietly, looking down at her plimsolls.

'Of course you could,' replies Mo just as quietly, for they have reached the hallway by now.

'I have my homework to do in the evenings,' replies Philippa, glancing at Mo's face.

191

'I'll help you do your homework. Then we'll have plenty of time to do it.'

'OK,' says Philippa finally, tossing the hair out of her eyes. 'I'll come up and see you after tea.' With that she puts a cautionary finger to her lips and, grasping the knob of the living-room door, swings herself out of sight as Mo, smiling to himself, climbs the stairs to his room.

Later that night, low voices and muffled sounds can be heard coming from Mo's room. At ten o'clock precisely the door opens, and Mo, after checking that all is clear, ushers Philippa out on to the landing from whence she tiptoes down the stairs. Every evening for the rest of that week Philippa continues to go to Mo's room, leaving punctually and unobserved at 10 p.m. – until Friday. Lucretia thinks she's heard something odd going on upstairs during the week. It's clear enough now, however. Grunts and groans, a few heavy thuds, coupled with shrieks of girlish delight, cause her finally to throw down the herbal chart she's been studying and rush upstairs to investigate, barging headlong into Mo's room.

She immediately finds the cause of the disturbance. Mo is standing over her daughter's outstretched body, which is lying along a black vinyl-cushioned bench. Her legs, gently spread, barely touch the floor, forcing her to point her toes downwards in order to gain leverage. Lucretia stares in amazement, first at her daughter, then at Mo, and back again to her daughter. Philippa is trying, accompanied by words of encouragement from Mo, to push a gleaming, chrome-handled, Multigym weight bar off her chest, groaning with frustration as she marshals all her strength for one last try. But the bar will not budge. Engrossed, they continue to ignore Lucretia's presence.

'It's OK. You did well to lift it once,' says Mo, picking up a towel and dabbing gently at the beads of perspiration covering Philippa's face, as Lucretia continues to stare in dumb immobility.

'I feel really light-headed,' says Philippa, sitting up, adding in an excess of enthusiasm as she glances at

Lucretia, 'and I'm not so terribly weak as I used to be. Why don't you have a go, Mummy?'

'Yes,' joins in Mo, 'your turn next, Lucretia.'

Lucretia isn't sure, she would prefer not to but she is more than a little fascinated by the flushed look of well-being on her daughter's normally pallid face. 'But it looks absolute torture. Do you really feel that much better now?' she enquires tentatively.

'Yes,' says Philippa. 'Oh, you don't know how wonderful it feels. Though I'm not able to stand up straight just yet. It really is a most marvellous experience.'

As Philippa is speaking, Lucretia is looking pensively at the Multigym. 'Well, it's quite obvious that we're going to have to figure out – and pretty soon – whether this machine, this . . .', she grimaces with dry tolerance, flicking her hand at the gym, 'this . . . apparatus really constitutes business or pleasure.'

'I would say it's always good business to improve the body and thereby the mind,' laughs Mo, winking at Philippa, who begins laughing too.

'I'm afraid I really can't see the point of any merriment here.' Lucretia rounds on them. 'We shall have to be quite clear about this because it may affect your rent adversely. Even your security of tenure.'

'It will affect neither,' replies Mo, heedlessly.

'What!' Lucretia begins to bristle like a thwarted turkey-cock, spinning round and flapping her arms in the air. 'Oh, yes!' she shrieks. 'That macho machine will certainly have to go.'

Mo inclines his head respectfully. 'You'll need to talk to Philippa about that.' Lucretia looks from one to the other with a puzzled frown. 'Because I'm leaving,' says Mo.

'Oh, are we losing our lodger?' she cries in mock concern.

Mo looks directly at her. 'It shouldn't bring on any panicky turns. You're a professional.' Lucretia's eyes narrow with incomprehension and annoyance. 'At losing things,' adds Mo coldly.

Lucretia turns, pushing her hands into the pockets of her dress. 'So, you'll be taking the machine away as soon as you get fixed up,' she replies swiftly, trying to give the impression that she has missed the contempt in his tone.

'No, Mo will not be taking it anywhere.' Lucretia stares at her daughter questioningly. 'He's leaving it for me,' she smiles over to Mo. 'I know enough about things to be able to carry on without supervision now. I've got a clear idea of how I'm going to develop myself, what to aim for. Please let me finish,' says Philippa calmly, as Lucretia tries to break in.

Much later Mo leaves. Neither Lucretia nor her daughter hears the door close as, bag in hand, he walks away from the house.

Even though it is well past 5 a.m. all but one of the main-line station doors are still firmly locked. The duty copper is upstairs in the Briefing Room. The homeless ones – who have avoided detection – sleep on, curled or spread flat in every out-of-the-way spot they can find. British Transport Commission Officer B Division 125 (better known as old Kidney Kicker Klint) is becoming a little agitated as the sergeant's voice drones on with the monthly briefing. Klint is duty copper and as such is responsible today for the smooth running of the station, including the unlocking of doors.

'Let's dispense with the stupid stuff first,' says the sergeant, running his eyes over the dozen or so coppers seated smoking and drinking their early morning cuppa in front of him. 'Fed up travellers,' continues the sergeant wearily. 'Three major grumbles which I shan't bother to go too deeply into here as they're outlined in the letter to the London Regional Transport Executive which is pinned on the bulletin board. Item 1: walls and ledges disgustingly filthy. Item 2: half the escalators out of order. Item 3: poor services, eleven drivers off sick. Not our concern. Tough shit, Joe Public.' This causes a laugh and paves the way into what should concern them. 'OK, Constable Klint. You'd better go.'

The trains for the south leave Glasgow Central on the hour, every hour. And the five forty-five coming in from the north is right on time as she speeds through Watford. The five forty-five (or as every trainspotter, young or old, from Dover to Dundee knows her, the *Pride of the Hebrides*) slows as she nears the terminus. Her passengers, suddenly aware of the drop in speed, let out a raucous cheer which cuts through the ticket collector's crap. Before their arrival shop shutters had clacked together to save glass that might be cracked by the wrath of the tartan army.

Someone hands the sergeant a cup of tea. After a sip he smacks his lips appreciatively. It is laced with rum as is everyone else's in the Briefing Room. They are going to need much fortification before this shift is out.

The sergeant smiles inwardly. Soon he will be away from all this. And isn't he entitled to smile because his years of unbiased integrity are about to be rewarded? Astute senior officers at Scotland Yard, having seen the potential of this future gem in their Metropolitan crown, are about to transfer him. He feels joyous, and perhaps a little honoured too, for on 1 June his new job will be at the newly formed Police Complaints Bureau, where his superiors feel sure he will set a shining example as Head of Ethnic Relations.

'OK. Let's get down to the main business of the day,' says the sergeant. 'It's that time of the year again, lads.' A dozen strained faces look at him. Beating up helpless old winos is one thing but young fit football fans . . . They all shift in their chairs, embarrassed to look at one another, frightened to see the fear in each other's eyes. All the flash talk and brave wisecracking ceases.

'OK. Everybody sitting comfortably? Then I'll begin,' continues the sergeant, trying to put a brave face on it. 'We had some very dodgy scenes here this time last year as those of you who were with me then will no doubt remember.' Someone replenishes his cup. 'Constable Pickon got a bruise on his left forearm as I remember – well, never forget, Hendon-trained stands to a good copper.' He allows himself a smile. 'Constable Duzem suffered a very painful wound when the top of his thumbnail got caught in one of the animals' scarves.' They all shake their heads in unison seriously at the thought.

'Yes,' goes on the sergeant, 'not very funny when you're off sick for a month or so, bored to death, champing at the bit, twiddling your thumbs in forced idleness. So we want to try and avoid a repetition of last year. For those of you who don't remember last year I'll refresh your memories.' And he does, reeling off a catalogue of carnage that if only half of it were true would have put Genghis Khan, Conan the Barbarian and all the generals in the British Army to shame.

He is interrupted by the voice of PC Klint, who has abandoned any attempt at formal police procedure and is shouting to the sergeant excitedly over the two-way radio like a youngster to his father. 'Sarge. Sarge. I'm down on the Victoria Line. Some of the passengers have been forced to flee across the live rails. These piss-pot fans are ripping up the platform benches, chocolate machines and litter bins. They're hurling them at the rival supporters. The driver's terrified. Yes. He's just abandoned the train to them, sarge. They've blocked the doors with seat cushions.'

'OK. OK. Keep calm.' He looks round at the others in the room. 'We've got them now. That's hijacking. We can hold the ring-leaders on the same charges as the Great Train Robbers faced.' The sergeant glimpses his moment of television glory here. 'Rule 8, Paragraph 9, Sub-section 11, "It is an offence to obstruct any train."' The sergeant is rubbing his hands with glee. 'A lot of improvisation and creativity in the Force has been lost since the sus laws were dropped. Now, when it quietens down I want you to go out and nick the ring-leaders, lads.'

'How will we know them, sarge?' asks one of the rookies, notebook in hand.

'Do me a favour. What were you studying at training college, lad? The humanities? Anyone you find drunk with a Scotch accent . . .'

The radio crackles. 'Sarge. A woman with a babe in arms has just jumped panicstricken down on to the rails and I don't know how many more commuters are trapped screaming between the rival fans on the platform.'

'OK. Leave it to me,' says the sergeant bravely. 'I'll speak to them.'

'You're not going out there, are you, sarge?' asks a clearly shocked young constable.

The sergeant looks smug. 'All part of the training, son.

Thirty years in the Force. You learn things. Not to worry, the British public will always rally to a good leader. I'd retire without my pension if I ever thought any of my officers was frightened by a handful of Scotch piss-pots.'

The young rookie, unsure how the remark is meant, begins to shake his head vigorously, as if to say he will never be guilty of such a thing. His face taking on a look somewhere between religious adoration and adolescent hero-worship, he continues to gaze at his sergeant, considering anew all the implications of what single-handedly he has threatened to do. The brave waiting on the brave.

Klint's voice breaks in loudly over the radio. 'Sarge! Sarge! The woman has fallen on the live rail, dropped the baby. Everything's gone mad!' During this report, in the background, were heard clearly the words of the traditional chant, 'Here we go. Here we go. Here we go', the rival faction replying with, 'Kill. Kill. Kill.'

The sergeant's face becomes twisted with fury. Like an old Norman warlord reaching for his sword, he grabs the Tannoy. His words are slow and precise. 'OK. Do not panic. I repeat. Do not panic. Passengers going about their lawful duties have nothing to fear. Remain calm at all times.' He takes another tot of rum, settling back in his chair with a look of professional weariness. 'Everything is under control . . .'

Over in another crowded but comparatively peaceful zone, Mo stands waiting as, technology brutalising his voice, the announcer drones instructions concerning a delay. A fading fluorescent strip flickers and struggles to remain alive. The stink of fumigants pierces Mo's senses. Bracing slightly, he lips a curse. A group of passengers on his right laugh at some remark, loudly and often elaborately proving that they are not miserable. Screech-crawling, the train inches along. Suddenly, getting the all clear, it shoots from the tunnel, braking with a rush of wind that gusts women's dresses up around their legs. The crowds, muscles tensed and shoulders hunched, begin the drudge scuttle: those trying to get on fight those trying to get off. In the fierce struggle someone stumbles against a child sucking an ice cream, which jams into its little face.

By side-scuttling around standers near the door, Mo manages to board swiftly as the child's mother bit into the offending passenger's arm. Nobody bothers with introductions as a couple of young females grab a man barring their way. Yoking him round the neck, they propel him forward like a battering ram to force a way on board as the doors close with a whispering swish and the train moves off.

Someone opens a vent to catch the cooling motion breeze, but as the train goes faster the breeze becomes colder, harder, stiffer, whipping the face.

To double-check the date Mo glances at the news-stand as he comes out of the station. Over the years, hundreds of headlines have screamed out their hype. 'Millions Killed in Quake'. 'Schoolchildren Die In Crash'. 'Bodies Mangled In Explosion'. 'Families Burnt To Death'. Meaningless words, instantly forgotten – unless we are involved. Mo checks the date. Monday 8 May. He peers at the large black type, each letter standing out bold and clear, forming words that speak to him.

Passengers Found Dead In Lift

Police last night launched an investigation into the deaths of nineteen commuters some of whom had horrific injuries to their fingers and hands resulting from their frantic efforts to avoid suffocation in the packed lift as they tried to prise open the doors. Fingernails were chipped and split, some down to the quick. Police and tube staff are still puzzled why no one heard the lift's alarm bell ring. After checking with engineers that it had suffered no mechanical or electrical fault, detectives told reporters they could find no cause and that the lift's mysteriously blocked doors are classed by insurance companies as an Act of God.

The paper was full of it, high on a raw voltage of sleaze.

Stuffing the paper into his pocket, mind racing to cover all the odds, Mo walks slowly away.

200